AF431335

GHOSTLY LEGENDS

Folklore of Southeastern Ohio

Lawrence Everett

Copyright © 2020 Lawrence Everett

All rights reserved. This book or any portion thereof may not be reproduced or used in any manner whatsoever without the express written permission of the publisher except for the use of brief quotations in a book review or scholarly journal. First Printing of Ghostly Legends: 2020 through Stormgate Press
ISBN: 9798647743473
Imprint: Independently published
stormgatepress.com
stormgatepress@gmail.com

CONTENTS

GHOSTLY LEGENDS
Folklore of Southeastern Ohio

Lawrence Everett

ACKNOWLEDGMENTS

I would like to thank the following people who made this revised and updated book possible. They were either involved in the original published works or in this revised edition.

Gavin Dillon, Amanda Dillon, Dwight Everett, Vikki Everett, Charles F. Millhouse, Millie Morrison, Paul Roof, Roger Perez
The Archives & Special Editions of Alden Library
The Mothman Museum, Point Pleasant, W.V.

A special thanks to Rachel Andrews for posing for the title page and back cover.

Damián Avilés for supplying the front cover art.

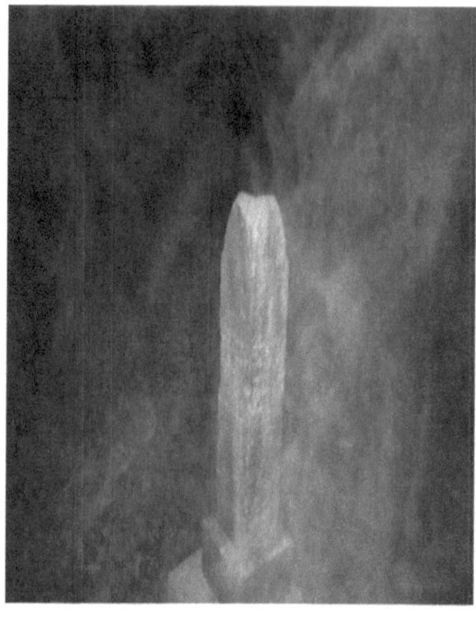

We thrive on reviews, good or bad. Please leave a review where you bought this book, or on goodreads.com

DEDICATION

13

I WOULD LIKE TO DEDICATE THIS BOOK
TO THE FOLLOWING INDIVIDUALS:

My Father, Dwight Everett, for passing down the family ghost stories and for helping me with the first two versions of this book.

My Grandson, Gavin Dillon, being the fourth generation to support the hunt for these legends and folklore.

Also, From Stormgate Press

The Captain Hawklin Adventure Series

The Secrets of Monster Island
The Subterranean Empire
The Jade Dragon
The Underwater Menace
The Lost Land
The Ghost Army (coming summer 2020)
The Shadow Men
The Skyhook Pirates

The New Kingdom Trilogy

Creatures of Habit
Daybreak Reckoning

The Origin Trilogy

Origin Expedition
Origin Equation
Origin Exodus (coming soon)

Visit stormgatepress.com for all available titles.

FORWARD

George Lucas once said, "Stories are never finished, just abandoned." While that statement is true, it is also true that stories can be revisited, much like Mr. Lucas did with his Star Wars trilogy.

Lawrence Everett has seized the opportunity to revisit his past works by updating, and focusing on his previous two books, "Ghost Spirits and Legends of Southeastern Ohio" and "Ghost and Legends of Southeastern Ohio and Beyond", into one book, "Ghostly Legends".

The stories in this edition have been re-edited while keeping the colloquialism of the accounts intact. While it is important to update his two previous efforts, there is a sense of updating and making this volume better than the others, and I believe we have achieved that.

Lawrence is a man of many talents. Outdoorsman, carpenter, inventor, ghost hunter, storyteller – a jack of all trades but master of none. He is a good friend, and though he might not admit it, an all-around nice guy. When he asked me to help him produce this book (After some persuasion on my part), I knew that most of the work would be done by Lawrence himself. He is a take charge kind of guy that won't allow anyone to do the hard work, that he could have done himself.

I'm happy that Stormgate Press has the opportunity to bring these stories back to a new generation of supernatural enthusiasts. To retell the accounts of Athens and Southeastern Ohio as told by past generations and now

passed down to you.
Charles F. Millhouse
Author, Publisher, Stormgate Press
May 2020

INTRODUCTION

It is known that Athens, Ohio is a special place for supernatural occurrences. There are many legends in this community. Are they truth or fiction? We may never know. I have heard these stories all my life and have even experienced a few. This book is a revised edition to my earlier publications Ghosts, Spirits and Legends of Southeastern Ohio, and Ghosts and Legends of Southeastern Ohio and Beyond published in 2002 and 2003. I visited these places many years ago. People are no longer allowed to visit most of these sites anymore. I have always taken a camera on these adventures in the hopes of catching a ghost, specter, or creature on film. Some of the stories or legends have been printed in local newspapers and magazines. Alden Library on the campus of Ohio University, (OU) also has a file on myths and legends in the archives and special collections (spook file). They have a lot of fascinating newspaper articles to read. There have also been stories published in other books over the years. I have no intention of disrespecting the authors who have written about these legends in the past. I have done a lot of research on the pentagram that surrounds Athens, Ohio. The pentagram looks attractive on a map but is it true or just another legend? You decide. I just wanted to see if it actually shows on a map. The main thing I noticed about mapping cemeteries is that there are several, that make smaller pentagrams. The question is: was this by accident or by design? Again, it is up to you to decide. Paranormal experiences seem more common than I first thought. A lot of people came forward with their own ex-

periences in my original publications, and I have retained those accounts as they were originally written by non-writers, to preserve the authenticity. Some of the accounts are from beyond Ohio. Including Kentucky, West Virginia and even a story from Toronto Ontario Canada. There seems to be a lot of spooks around the country and even other interesting things like the Mothman in Point Pleasant, West Virginia, Bigfoot in the Western United States and Canada and even UFO's from beyond. I have chronicled my own experiences and other unexplained phenomena in this book. It seems that anything can create a legend or myth. Each person has to decide if they believe it or not. There are a lot of ghosts that haunt the OU campus buildings, in Athens, Ohio I have vaguely covered them for they have been published in other works, and I didn't want to infringe or disrespect previous author's work. I have visited some homes that were claimed to be haunted or weird things that happened in or around them. I have taken some photos in which appeared orbs. Orbs are one of the most photographed anomalies. Are these anomalies captured on film really ghosts or just some strange reaction of the camera or maybe dust particles? I have seen and photographed some of them, but I am still a skeptic on whether they are real or not. Ghost hunting and mysterious creatures have become a lot more popular since these stories were originally published. From the beginning of time and civilization was just getting started there have been ghost stories. Even in these modern, social media times, there will always be legends and folklore, enjoy the retelling of these ghost stories and legends.
Lawrence Everett 2020

SEEDS OF LEGENDS

As the golden glow of the sun makes way for the silver aura of the moon, All is sure that the midnight hour is soon, A flicker of light, a hush, a quiet countenance of gloom, A spirit from the past leaves its tomb, A wailing apparition enters the room, A specter appears with a chilling air and a paralyzing fear of doom, A racing heartbeat is beginning to zoom, A sudden clap of thunder makes a gigantic boom, After all is over, the seeds of legends come into bloom.
Lawrence Everett 2001

TALE OF A LEGEND

On all Hallows Eve in the dead of night a mist shadowed moon will begin to glow, Supernatural occurrences are sure to show, Howling hounds will be the sound of impending doom as the chill of the night wind begins to blow, Ghosts and ghouls are seen rising out of their graves and tombs from six feet below, Chills creep up your spine as the rise of the dead is slow, Terror strikes your heart and the body is so frozen with fear that you can't move a toe, Fear that it is your time to feel the Grim Reapers touch with your spirit in his tow, As soon as the brush with death passes and all is well as rays of the sunshine over the hills low, This will become the start of a legend you can begin to sow, The legend of a midnight hour horror tale for all to know.
Lawrence Everett 2003

Ghosts

THE SIMMS LEGEND

When it's close to Halloween, Athens, Ohio will have its annual block party, which draws people from everywhere. There are other things that draw people to Athens, such as the legends that surround the community. The five cemeteries, that form a pentagram, is one legend, they are Simms, Hanning, Cuckler, Higgins and Zion. Athens has a ghostly legend about Simms Cemetery; the legend states the Judge Simms was a hanging judge and hung the convicts in the cemetery. It has a rock cliff on the right side from which a tree protrudes that was used to hang people according to the legend.

The rope scars can still be seen. I have been there and the oak tree that extends over the cliff does look like it has rope scars on the limbs. All my life I have heard of hauntings around that area. There is also mention of an eerie robed figure not allowing people entrance into the cemetery. The legends are never put to rest; they always seem to come up in some conversation. There are rumors of tombstones being turned over, but mysteriously they are put back in place. Was Judge Simms putting them back, or was some stranger coming in and putting them back?

I don't know the answers to these questions, but the only thing I can say for sure is the rope burns are in the tree. I have heard that a lot of people have seen ghosts in the area, could they be Simms victims, or is the old Judge still walking the ground cursed for eternity?

THE GHOST OF THE TUNNEL

The ghost of the Moonville Tunnel is one of those legends that's based on certain truth. The story has changed over the years, but the most popular tale goes something like this: Back in the early 1900's a man was killed by a train in the tunnel and his spirit forever haunts the tracks. The Moonville Tunnel is located in Zalaski State Forest; I have visited the Moonville Tunnel several times and have yet to see any ghosts. The last time I visited, the only really weird thing that happened was the freezing chill, kind of like the one my wife and I felt at Hanning Cemetery. I first found the tunnel in the 1980s when a buddy and I were turkey hunting. I was fascinated. This was before I heard all the myths that are told of the tunnel. My first visit was incredible, because the trestle was still there and we could walk across the track. If a train was to come while I was there, what was I going to do? But none showed that day. Maybe because it was already an abandoned track, I don't know. Now I have read of engineers on the trains seeing the ghost in the tunnel when they were passing through. From the newspaper articles and people who have seen it, the ghost is described as being black, about eight feet tall with a white beard. His eyes glisten like balls of fire and he appears to be wearing a miner's hat. In one hand he holds a lantern and is dressed in dirty overalls. I have never seen this apparition and I don't think I want to. The legend says that it has to be storming out for the ghostly lantern to be seen. I have always been there on nice calm evenings and that is probably why I have never seen anything. The only thing that is really familiar about this legend is the light we have on our property. It will appear on stormy nights after a rain. After watching it roam the hills it makes your hair stand up on the back of your neck and a freezing chill run down your spine. I can only imagine the ghost of the tunnel would do more. There seems to be more ghosts around the tunnel. One of them is reported to be a girl who was killed when she was caught on the trestle by a train while going to visit a lover. The Moonville cemetery is haunted or at least that's the rumor; I think I would like to visit it to see if it is. I have wondered if the ghost of the tunnel is similar to the ghost on our property. I've wonder if it is a gas pocket that lights up , that would explain a lot of things. There are a lot of mine shafts in the Moonville area. I bet you could never convince the people who have seen the spirit. Whatever is out there I am sure we will never know. But the legend keeps getting stronger over the years and the tunnel will not be forgotten for a very long time.

A NIGHT AT MOONVILLE

It was a cold dark December evening; the moon was only shining about one quarter through the night sky. All was quiet as we were driving through Zaleski State Forest to get to the Moonville Tunnel. I was thinking that this is the night to see the Moonville ghost. One legend of the ghost is that he was having an affair with the wife of the engineer. When the engineer found out he decided to take matters in his own hands. One night as they were stopped on the tracks in the tunnel the engineer asked the conductor to check something under the train. When the conductor stuck his head under the train, the engineer moved it forward beheading him.

When we arrived, we had to walk the narrow path along

Raccoon Creek to get to the tunnel. We topped a little hill to the old railroad bed and to our left was the tunnel entrance. It was so dark a person couldn't see the other end of the tunnel even with our flashlights. I have heard the legend of the headless conductor many times over the years and even wrote some on it in this book. My friend Chuck and I have been to the tunnel many times in the daylight hours. This was the first time either of us had been here in the nighttime. We brought our cameras and video cameras in the hopes of catching the conductor swinging his lantern in the tunnel.

We ventured down through the tunnel looking at the bricks and the graffiti on the walls. Quietly listening to the wind blowing and howling in the tunnel. We took photos and video taped for about 25 minutes.

The ghostly lantern was not meant to be seen on this night. The only lantern we saw was part of the graffiti on the walls. On our way out of the tunnel lights appeared across from where the trestle once stood. We both froze in our tracks for a minute. It was only someone parking a vehicle.

After returning to our vehicle we decided we hadn't had enough for the night. So away we went to the Moonville Cemetery. Where the headless conductor is rumored to be buried. Once we arrived there and got out of the vehicle it was an eerie feeling of being watched. Unknown to me at this time Chuck also had the same feeling. We walked into the cemetery snapping photos and videotaping. When suddenly Chuck found a cold spot, it was really cold. Colder than the December night air we had been exposed to.

As I was taking photos, I walked past the video camera when Chuck started to freak out a little. A ball of light was following me. This is what ghost hunters call an orb. We had decided that was enough for the night. Chuck left his video camera on till we got to our vehicle. On our way home we were discussing the feeling of being watched. After viewing our video, we found two more orbs had followed us to our vehicle. One was really bright and the other was kind of a yellow color. I am somewhat of a skeptic on this filming of orbs, but I have no explanation of what is was. I have to wonder, were we being watched by the orbs, or were we escorted from the cemetery?

SPIRITS OF THE PAST

When Halloween comes everyone starts thinking about ghosts. This makes me think of the ghosts and spirits that linger around our home and our farm. One for instance is an eerie light that appears on a hillside across from our house. It will get really bright then just fade into the night. Is this what legends call a banshee or will-o-the-wisp? This light has been appearing off and on for over a hundred years.

My grandmother, my dad, and I too have seen this eerie light. I myself have never ventured to see just what exactly this light is, but my dad did about thirty years back. However, he didn't speak much of it because I don't think he liked what he came across. My wife has seen this light as well. Sometimes there is more than one that seems to make a line across the ridges. We very seldom talk of this to strangers, but the ones we have talked to seem to think the lights are pockets of gas that light up, also known as St. Elmo's Fire. My father thinks differently. I myself am happy with the gas pocket theory, because I don't think I want to follow in his footsteps to see just what it is.

There is also a spirit that has wandered around our house and the house that was once built on this spot. It is my great aunt's spirit, who seems to be watching over us. Back in the 1950's she died an unexpected death while living on the family farm. We have heard her walking around our house and my wife has also seen her ghostly image standing in our yard, not too far from the pear tree. Just like when she lived, she is dressed in black, or at least my father said that was how she was dressed when she was buried. She was known to linger on this very spot in the farmhouse before the present house. The reason why we believe it is her spirit in our house is because just like my great aunt, the spirit likes to tickle our feet. The weirdest part of it is, when your feet are being tickled you can't move, you just lie there and take it. The worst part of this experience is that it feels like sharp fingernails or maybe the finger bones of a skeleton that can't be seen.

Also, every once in while a person can hear low voices talking gibberish in the house. They can almost be understood but it happens so fast it is like it never happened. We can sit on the porch and hear this when all else is quiet. The other weird thing is books will fly off shelves, but it is only certain books, it is as if someone doesn't like this particular type of book. There have been instances of specters being seen in the bathroom and at the end of our beds just watching over us, one is a woman and the other is a man dressed in black.

One time when I was working in the garage I turned around just in time to see a ghostly apparition wearing bib overalls watching me, but he just vanished into nothing like he was never there, it sure did make cold chills go all over my body. Another encounter that happened in the garage was my father and a guest came one evening to go in it to look at something; when my father opened the door someone tapped him on the shoulder, but when he turned no one was there and his guest was still in the car. Was he being warned not to take his buddy in the garage? No one knows for sure, except the ghost who tapped him on the shoulder.

One time I told my buddy Chuck about the light that appears on our farm, so he wanted to see. We traveled to the farm every night for a week, but the light never appeared for him to see. On our way back an eerie occurrence happened. We turned off the road and a white ghostly form went in front of our vehicle floating about four feet off the ground, it appeared to have the form of a woman. I started to ask Chuck if he had seen it, but before I could get the words out, he said "Let's get the hell out of here and make it fast." It made the hair on the back of our necks stand straight on end. Even with the experiences I have had, I never believed in ghosts until I moved back here on our family farm and have experienced many things in our house. I would never talk about these experiences until my wife and stepdaughter came to me and spoke of their own experiences in this house, which which was the same as mine.

WILLO-THE-WISP

There is a light that burns in each of our fields that looks like a kerosene lantern burning. The light looks to come up out of the ground, it glows really bright then it travels for about twenty feet then stops. The glow then dims till it disappears. Sometimes it will happen eight or ten times a night, after that it might not show up for three weeks. One night a friend and I went over to it when the moon was full and bright. Suddenly, the moon disappeared under the clouds and everything got real dark. So, we were standing there wondering what to do next while all was still and dark.

Then all at once something came dragging down through the field; it sounded like someone pulling a chain. We couldn't see what it was because it was too dark, but it was moving about six feet in front of us, so we decided it was best to get away from there. We took off running and ran into a big briar patch, it ripped our clothes up pretty good. It was too dark to tell, but my first thought was "this is the end," I'm caught by this thing, but lucky for us it was only the briars. We never did go back over to see the light again. I decided it was best to view this lantern type light burning bright from afar.

All the neighbors have seen this light. We used to watch it come across the hill while we were milking the cows. This light has been appearing for over a hundred years, my grandfather and my mother saw it. Some people have said that gas acts like that, but I often wonder if the gas sounds like a chain dragging too.

36

SPECTER FROM THE PAST

On a road near New Marshfield, upon a ridge sets Haines Cemetery, peaceful and quiet. In this cemetery lies the spirit of a Civil War officer who went crazy. His war deeds drove him to destroy his home near the graveyard on Halloween Eve. Sometime after he returned home, he attacked his family and set fire to their house, killing himself and his family in the process.

Their bodies were buried in Haines Cemetery where his spirit can reportedly be seen roaming restlessly. This is the legend that surrounds this cemetery. My wife and I went to visit this cemetery on Halloween to see if we could see the specter hanging around. Some part of the legend that I have heard is that he is riding his horse -- even in this century.

This is one of the reasons we went. I could just imagine

seeing a Civil War specter riding down that ridge --just thinking of seeing it makes cold chills roll over my body. Just imagine something like that happening as a person rounded the curve to get to the cemetery. Worse yet, would be seeing it while you were away from your vehicle. Seeing the spirit would be very interesting, but to see the horse too? The adrenaline would definitely be on overload for a sight like that. A person's hair would look probably like a perm gone bad, standing straight up.

We did not see any spirits that evening. Was it luck that we didn't or misfortune? It could have been luck; I don't think that a heart attack from seeing a Civil War specter would be incredibly good; especially if the spirit is still crazy, or angry because the living is trespassing on his territory.

One of the other reasons we went there was this cemetery is part of a pentagram that surrounds Athens. I have been checking these out on a map. I would like to visit them all. I guess there are two legends that go with this cemetery. They are the pentagram and the Civil War officer's ghost. This is just another sample of the folklore that surrounds this area of Athens. Fact or fiction is for someone else to decide, I'm only the storyteller. This was my experience on this ridge.

OUR FRIENDLY FARMHOUSE GHOST
Eyewitness account

There are many legends around Athens County, Ohio regarding spirits or ghosts. This is not a legend, but a documentation of a personal encounter with such an entity. In 1965, my husband David, five children, and I moved into a seven-room farmhouse in Millfield, Ohio, that was built around 1863. We had heard the house was haunted; I was thrilled with the prospect. Former residents had told me they felt a presence, but evidently it was a "friendly ghost" as nothing totally diabolical ever occurred. Everyone who had lived there had minor problems with vacuum cleaners, water pumps, "things going bump in the night," and the constant leaking ceiling in the kitchen when it rained. Every family had tried to repair the roof over the kitchen, but never could find or fix the hole. Even David had the roof repaired, but as far as I know, it still leaks to this day.

David's aunt Goldie, born in 1899, was raised in the next farmhouse up the hill. Many of her answers to my questions filled in some of the blanks regarding this entity. There were several suggestions: the house at one time had been a nursing home, but when the residents were sick, they were taken to Sheltering Arms Hospital or the Athens State Hospital in Athens, Ohio. No one knew for sure if anyone had died in the house. I attempted to communicate with the entity, and never felt the nursing home resident theory was right. I always felt it was more of a violent death that had occurred in the kitchen. I asked Aunt Goldie and she remembered that when she was quite young there was a peddler who traveled the country roads with a horse-drawn wagon selling household items: pots and pans, needles and thread, bolts of material, soaps, perfumes, etc. He would come every few months, and sometimes would be invited into the homes for a meal or a cool drink. One day, he just didn't show up anymore, and when the farmers got to talking about him, they realized the last place he was seen was at our farmhouse on Bell Road. Goldie said there were several stories about what happened, and no one was really telling the truth. Evidently, as one story goes, the peddler went to that home to peddle his goods, was invited into the house, and was shot in the pantry (the room we used as the kitchen). The story goes that he was then put into the well, and a barn or corncrib was built over the well. Another story was the peddler was invited to stay overnight, they were having a dance, and he got into an argument with one of the music makers (perhaps the guitar player). Anyway, he was killed in the pantry, left there until the next day, and then buried somewhere on the farm, or maybe thrown into the well.

If the peddler arrived at a farmhouse around suppertime – it was the custom to invite him to stay and eat with them; if it were too late, he would stay overnight, usually sleeping in the barn with this horse and wagon, and leaving early the next morning without anyone knowing it. That's why no one suspected anything when he didn't show up at the next farmhouse – they just assumed he had gone elsewhere at daylight. Evidently, he never lived through that night. No one knew, except the people involved, exactly what took place that fateful night.

Over the course of time that we lived there, whenever I was alone cleaning house, doing chores, working crossword puzzles, and even while sleeping, things would come to my mind regarding "my ghost." I called him several names, but somehow "Jeremiah" was the only name that seemed right. I'm not sure I communicated with him, as I have no experience in that field, but whenever I'd go over some course of action regarding his death, some things just came to my mind on their own and just seemed right.

We had several incidents and "happenings" that I attributed to Jeremiah. The first month or so, we learned that our ghost did not like guitars. David was building a closet in the parlor that would become our bedroom. I had placed my dad's guitar on the shelf – the only thing in the closet – I was ironing, and the kids were lying on the bed. We were just talking, no one was rowdy, the weather was a warm, pleasant summer day, and suddenly the guitar came flying out of the closet and hit the foot of the bed, a good two feet away, and shattered. The kids and I just watched. There was nothing else in the closet that would have caused the guitar to slide off the shelf; there was no wind, no tremor, nothing – and the distance from the closet to the bed was not close enough for the guitar to just slip off the shelf.

I believe that was our first true encounter. For years to come, every time someone played a guitar in the house, they had broken strings. A few of them just changed strings and would start to play, but again, the strings would break. They could play on the porch or out in the yard without problems. Other stringed instruments were not bothered; we would hold square dances in the dining room on occasion with a mandolin, fiddle, and banjo, but no guitars.

We had a clock hanging on the wall in one corner of the kitchen after a few weeks, the hands would always be at 6:30. We would reset the clock, but again, 6:30. So we'd buy a new clock. Sometimes the clock would last for several months, and sometimes only a few weeks. Once Vikki, our oldest daughter, had a male friend over and was telling him about "our ghost," she said the clock would just go to 6:30 and stay there. He didn't believe her, and said he thought she was nuts. About that time, the glass came off the clock and flew onto the kitchen table, which was several feet from the wall. Needless to say, he got up and left. . . he never did come back.

Jeremiah also didn't like the vacuum cleaner, he didn't like the water pump, and he didn't like the clock hanging on that one wall in the kitchen. I had to come to an understanding with him so we could live there in peace. I let him know that there was room for all of us, but he had to behave himself. The kids were never afraid of him, they just talked to him and we all went about our merry way. After I moved the clock to the other wall, he never bothered it.

Our youngest daughter at age 12-13 had a slumber party one Friday night, I told her not to say anything about Jeremiah because I didn't want the girls scared (I also told Jeremiah to behave himself that night). They were all to sleep on the living room floor just a wall away from my bedroom. Around midnight, one of the girls suggested they hold a séance...I cringed, but thought, "What could it hurt?" they were getting pretty serious after a while and kept saying, "Give us a sign. . . stop the clock over the TV." The clock over the TV was like an old school-house clock with a swinging pendulum, I was afraid that Jeremiah would stop the clock, so I got up and told them it was late and they probably should forget the séance and go to sleep. Nothing more was thought about it. The next day, Saturday, the girl's parents got them early in the day and my kids just did "their thing." Later in the evening, the boys came into the house, looked at the clock over the TV and remarked that it was only 8:00 and they had time to shower and get ready for bed before Chips came on TV. About 10 minutes till nine, Chuck turned on the TV... Chips was just ending. Of course, the boys were angry that someone had messed with the clock. It was then that I and my daughter realized that Jeremiah had stopped the clock as requested the night before. I was mighty glad the girls did not notice it, or I would have had a bed full of 12-13-year-old girls.

There were several other "things" that went on, such as when the curtain in the living room was knocked off the rod: I couldn't reach it standing on a chair, so I climbed off the chair and said, "Okay, Jeremiah, I guess you got to fix this curtain." I walked away and didn't think any-thing about it. Later that night while we were watching TV, I noticed the curtain was fixed. I asked the kids if they hung it back up, and they said, "No," they hadn't even noticed when it was down. I reckon Jeremiah must have fixed it.

A few times we had guests that remarked they felt some-thing or someone in the house and asked if we had a "ghost." I always told them we did and introduced them to Jeremiah. Of course, a lot of people also thought we were all a "little strange."

When we moved, I offered to let Jeremiah move with us, but I don't think he did, as I had rented it to two boys, they stayed only one night. When I asked them why they didn't want to live there, the reply was, "Whoever is here doesn't like our lifestyle;" but they did not elaborate on what exactly took place.

I believe Jeremiah is still in the house, staying there alone. No one has lived there since.

JEREMIAH'S HAUNT

This is a visit to a house of a story previously written called "Our friendly farmhouse ghost". We were all curious to see if this entity still resided in this residence. As we were driving down the driveway to this old house there was a feeling of dread like something or someone was watching us. It probably didn't help with the big trees draping across the driveway. But the feeling of anxiety or uneasiness was there, nonetheless.

Upon arriving Babs, my mother-in-law, was already there sitting on the steps of the back porch. We were a group of five on this night. She had no problem informing us that Jeremiah was still there. She had her coffee cup lid taken off and her coffee dumped as she sat there and watched. We were standing around talking and trying to decide if we should continue this adventure or just go home and forget about it. All of a sudden Chuck's hat lifted off the video camera eyepiece and gently fell to the ground. It was almost like someone lifted it and laid it on the ground. Was this a sign not to wear the hat or not to go in at all? Well after this incident we decided to go anyway. Babs went straight to the kitchen were a lot of this entity's mischief was done. Every clock that was hung on the wall had been destroyed when she lived there.
We took a few photos of this area. This is what showed up in the photos. After looking around we went to the stairs where it was freezing cold at the bottom.

What was very eerie was the noises at the top of the steps. We all heard it but seen nothing. It was almost as if someone or something was moving around. We looked around for a long time in hopes we could see what had made the noises. Could this be Jeremiah? We were never to know because the noise stopped. When we went back downstairs, we decided to stop in the bedroom. This bedroom was also used as some kind of funeral parlor in the past. It was all quiet and very uneasy in this room. Wandering through this old house was a very fascinating experience. Were these photos we took and the mysterious and unexplainable things that had happened all part of overactive imaginations? We all heard the sounds and seen Chuck's hat moving.

As we were leaving, I walked over to the kitchen window for one last photo. I snapped the photo and never thought anymore about this picture until we viewed them. This is the photo. Is this a coincidence or is it Jeremiah watching us leave? Who is to say for sure?

MORBID PLANTER
Lady and the sinking drum

I had seen an article in the Sunday Messenger from October 20, 1962 about a murder case. It involved an Ohio University professor murdering his wife. The fact is he blacked out and went nuts then beat his wife in the head with a crowbar. He bent her in half and shoved her lifeless body in to a 55-gallon oil drum. He filled the drum with holes and took her to Dow Lake. Blanketed by darkness he stole a rowboat and went out in the lake and dropped the drum in the water. The police finally caught up with him and he pleaded guilty to the crime. The professor was sentenced for a very long jail term. But he escaped and has been on the run ever since. I remember my dad talking about this when I was very young. I think the whole community was in an uproar about the murder. This all happened back in 1962, and I think it gets brought up about once a year around my house.

These are the facts that really happened. But like every-thing else in this community there now resides a legend about it. The legend is the drum that was used to sink her body in the lake was dotted with holes. It is rumored to be used as a flowerpot in the front yard of an Athens residence. It never leaks no matter how much water is poured into it. Originally, the professor used this drum to dispose of his wife's body in Dow Lake after he killed her. I have heard of this legend before and would like to see if it is true. The question I have -- is the drum still in good shape after all these years and not rusted away?

I can't deny that this legend isn't true. I just think it is a neat aspect like the rest of the legends that surround Athens, Ohio. It goes hand in hand with all the unusual things that happen around the community. I have been investigating some of these legends and would like to see this one.

GEORGE'S PRESENCE
Eyewitness Account

A lot of weird things happened in this old house that we lived in, in Nelsonville Ohio. TVs and radios would power on and off with nobody around. The house had a stairway with twelve steps that would lead a person to the upstairs. Anyone that came to visit always said they had no problem with steps; anytime those words were spoken they either would fall going up or coming down the steps. For some reason or another you would trip when traversing the stairs, nothing is ever seen or felt by anyone. Every time something happened,

I am not sure I can say what it was, but I think there was a spirit in the house. There were times you could feel a presence, but we never heard any sounds. We gave this spirit the name of George. We were able to catch a picture of George, when a friend was taking a picture of my cat.

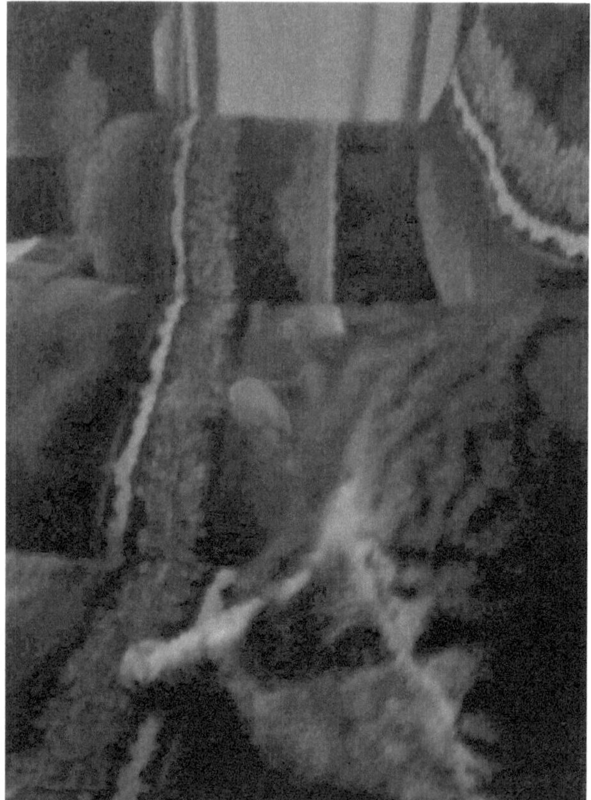

The first photo was just the cat, then the second photo showed George standing there watching us. It was exciting and eerie at the same time to know that George was in our presence. I have since moved from this house, but will George be there for the next family?

THE CRYING BABE

On a hilltop is a cemetery not too far from Stroud's Run State Park. There are several graves. When I was a kid my friend lived in a house at the bottom of the hill. We were always playing around his house goofing off and being kids. He was quite a practical joker and one evening his jokes came to an end. I was in his garage when he came running from the back of the house. He was so scared his face was white as death. Jokingly, I asked if he had heard the dead? Boy was I right! He heard a baby crying in the cemetery on top of the hill. It was as plain as day, and we knew the cemetery was empty -- only the dead were there, and there was a baby buried in that cemetery.

THE VANISHING COUPLE
Eyewitness Account

One night while driving past an old country cemetery, I seen a man and woman walking along the driveway to the cemetery. I never thought anything about it until I saw they had a glowing aura around them. I slowed down a little so I could watch them. They walked off the side of the drive and vanished into thin air. There are three incidents at that cemetery that I know of. The name of this cemetery I don't want to reveal because there are still relatives living not to far from it. There seems to a specter or legend around every cemetery, or so I have found out. I wonder if anyone else has seen more than they bargained for? I probably will never know why or who the couple was. I know my experiences scared me really bad. I would almost bet that I had the same look of death-warmed-over that my friend had the night he heard the baby cry from the same cemetery.

GRANDMA'S VOICE
Eyewitness Account

About three weeks after my grandmother died, my aunt and I were sitting upstairs in our old farmhouse, the kitchen at that time was in the basement. We were just sitting around talking. I was a lot younger; this was when World War II was almost over. I got the call to be drafted and was ready to leave any day. I told my aunt I was getting ready to leave for the war when all of a sudden, a spirit talked from the basement and said, "Oh my no", It was my grandmother's voice. That was the first and only spirit I ever heard speak in my life.

FOOTFALLS
Eyewitness Account

After my aunt died, I came home from work, it was a long hot day, so I just sat on the porch. I never bothered to turn on any lights in the house, a neighbor stopped by for a visit, so I invited him to sit on the porch for a spell. We sat there for a while when my guest spoke up and said, "You have a woman in the house!" I told him no, I was the only one there. He said there is a woman in there because I can tell the footfalls are that of a woman. I had heard the same thing, but I kept quiet about it. He kept insisting that someone was in there. So, we went in and looked all over the house even under the beds. We found nothing, but I knew it was my aunt because she would walk from the mirror to the bed where she slept when she was alive. I knew for sure it was her from the way she walked and where the footsteps went. This happened in the 1950s, about two to three weeks after she died. I was shocked that my guest could hear her footfalls, but not as shocked as he was to hear them himself.

Another appearance of my aunt happened after I got married. My wife and I slept in the same room that my Aunt did when she was alive. My wife always had a habit of looking out the window before she went to bed. She pulled the curtain back and glanced out the window, the moon was shining bright on this night. I was getting ready to climb into bed when she yelled, "Oh my, come here quick -- there is a woman standing out here." I looked and could see nothing. My wife said the woman she saw standing out by the well had a black dress on.

This was the same kind of dress that the undertaker had put on my aunt. My aunt's spirit came back, but it wasn't for me to see it on that night. My wife also heard my grandmother and my aunt walking up the stairs crying, we had abandoned the basement, but she heard them several times; it got so bad that she refused to live there, and we moved.

UNINVITED GUEST
Eyewitness Account

My half-brother Bob came to stay with us one night and we had to share beds because there wasn't enough room for everyone. We were lying there and the only light we had was just a little bit shining from the living room. We couldn't see anything it was so dark in the bedroom. All of a sudden it felt like something stepped upon the bed and the bed mashed down, like when a person steps on the bed. This thing stepped over my leg and right over his leg and went right into the wall. We got up and turned on the light and found nothing, but he wouldn't sleep in the dark the rest of the night. I figure it was the spirit of the original owner of the house. This was not an isolated incident it happened to anyone who slept in that bedroom. So needless to say, no one liked to sleep in there with the light off. No one wanted the uninvited guest in the room.

FINAL RESTING PLACE
Eyewitness Account

One night I had a strange feeling someone was watching me. I sat straight up in the bed and standing at the foot of the bed, was a tall man. This man had shoulder length long black hair, was very tanned, and didn't have a shirt on, only blue jeans. He did not scare me even after he faded into nothing.

A few days later I told my father-in-law all about the apparition that had appeared. I described the man to him. He told me that it sounded like a guy who worked on the farm many years ago.

Months later while my husband and I were standing in our yard we noticed some vehicles pull down by our meadow. Several people got out of the vehicles. One gentleman was dressed completely in black and wore a black cowboy-type hat. This man was holding a white bag. We thought they were dumping trash out. We went to see what they were up to. The gentleman in black said his father had passed away a few months back and his father's final request was for his ashes to be scattered on this property because he used to work on this farm and loved being here. So, they scattered his ashes and left.

The man that scattered the ashes was tall and had black hair. He kind of resembled the apparition that I had seen. I told my father-in-law about this and we concluded that the man at the foot of the bed finally came to his final resting place.

A PICTURE OF GRANDMA
Eyewitness Account

Before David and I got married, his mother told me that David was "Grandma's little boy; that he could do no wrong, and there probably was never going to be a girl that would be good enough for him." I assured her that Grandma would like me! Once while sitting in the living room, the rocking chair that was in the corner started rocking with no one in it, no breeze blowing, and no other vibration to make it move. I told them it was Grandma and the chair stopped rocking. We got married in St. Mary's, West Virginia and didn't have a wedding or a reception, and the only wedding gift we received was a coffee pot from my boss. I took it in the house to show my in-laws, and then took a picture of "our wedding gift."

When the film was developed, there was a ghostly haze across the picture... I told them it was Grandma, letting me know that I was accepted. There was no one in the room when I took the picture, no one was smoking, and there was no other "means" for the haze. I felt quite comfortable thinking that it was Grandma . . . sometimes I'd even talk to her, especially if David and I didn't see eye-to-eye about some things, then I'd tell David that she was disappointed in him . . . Of course, they thought I was nuts!! My mother-in-law said that sometimes she had a feeling that someone was in the house but didn't want anyone to think she was crazy, so she never mentioned it. Grandma died in that house, as had Grandpa, but my mother-in-law never mentioned having any feeling of Grandpa being in the house. Of course, it was common knowledge that Grandma "ruled the roost" so to speak when she was living; maybe she wanted to do that also after death.

THE CORNER OF MY EYE
Eyewitness Account

There are work experiences that have been told many times about spooks and specters, mine may be no different but it has been asked of me to tell this tale to the best of my ability.

I work for an area business in Athens County, Ohio off US Route 33 that was built where an old farm sat at one time and many years before an old mill of some kind, of what I'm not sure. There have been many sightings, not only by me, of strange apparitions moving between doors, and cold chills running up your spine, but there has even been physical contact as well in the way of shoving and of something walking past.

There has even been completed work, undone overnight, causing much speculation as to how this happened. Lights suddenly appeared on after they were known to be shut off. What makes the encounters so interesting is that the building isn't incredibly old, so this makes one to believe that the spirit or spirits were there long before the building was constructed. I have no other leads to this, but it makes me wonder what things may have happened there on US Route 33.

THE EERIE APPARITION
Eyewitness Account

There was a house down across the road from the meadow where I used to round up the cows and bring them in for milking. As I went around the hill to find the cattle I could look straight down on to this abandoned house and the garden on the other side of it. The people that had lived there were dead and no one was supposed to be living there.

Once in a while I would see a woman out in this garden with braided hair. She would be working in it, her braided hair showed up really well for as far away as I was. There was a little man who would stand on the porch for a while then turn around and walk back into the house. One time we had a cross bull in the field and my uncle didn't want me going after the cattle alone, so he went with me to round them up. As we went around the hill my uncle said, "Stop and take a look at that, there is a little man who is coming out of that abandoned house and a woman in the garden."

The man wore a straw hat and I said to my uncle, "Let's get a little closer for a better look at this." We got as close as we dared and watched the little man who would go in and out of the house. We just sat on the side of the hill and watched them for the longest time. After a while they both went in together and we didn't see them come out. This eerie phenomenon happened about once a week, the first thing you would see is the woman out in the garden, and then the little man prancing back and forth, in and out of the house. It was like he didn't know whether to stay in or out. He was very nervous acting.

One time after watching this phenomenon we decided to go over to this house to see who was staying there. When we got to the house there was nothing or no one in inside. It was like these people or spirits had vanished from the face of the earth, after we had seen them go into the house. But within a week they would be back doing the same thing over and over again. My uncle and I could never find a trace of any people or ghosts in this abandoned house for we checked many times.

SEARCHING.........

Back around the 1940s an old man lived by himself not too far from Athens. His wife had passed away quite a while back. He started working away from home but always tried to get back in the evenings. One night when he came home the house caught on fire. How the fire started is as much of a mystery as to what happened to him that night. It was assumed he was brutally beaten furthermore robbed and all his money was taken from him. Then the robbers threw him into the burning house. What happened for sure no one knows, but the fact that he was dead.

Sometime after this happened, a person could travel down the road on a stormy evening near the house and see a brightly glowing lantern floating around the yard. Perhaps this was the spirit looking for the people who had murdered him or maybe looking for his lost money? The road that went by this house is no longer in use and hasn't been for roughly 40 years. The road has disappeared with the years of brush and foliage growing on it.

The house is long gone with the tragic effects of time. I often wonder if the lantern or spirit is even now floating around the place maybe still looking for the people who had possibly killed him so many years ago.

65

NIGHTLY TERROR
Eyewitness Account

There was a large old house in Athens, that if you opened the door to go upstairs, every once in a while, an apparition appeared at the top of the stairs.

  If someone were to sleep in the upstairs bedroom the covers would get pulled off of him or her. My grandmother used to tell that she could hear a thud on the floor like someone falling to it. She said some nights it was really bad and would occur more than once, it was hard to ignore that it was happening. Most of the people that visited the house or worked in it hated to go upstairs after night.

We had heard a rumor that one of the previous owners of the house shot himself there. Was this why the upstairs was haunted? I remember my grandmother telling me about all the happenings while she was there. I never went in to see or hear the ghost or spirit for myself. Her telling of it was enough to keep me away from there. The house is gone now with the advancement of modern civilization. I often wonder every time I drive by the structure that is built on that spot now, does it have the same occurrences as the house did, or did the ghost finally get to rest in peace. Maybe it haunts the halls of the building there now.

SCREAMING HOLLOW
Eyewitness Account

On or near Luhrig Road outside of Athens, Ohio there is a dead-end road on the top of a hill. Many years ago, a woman lived in the old house that was on this spot of land; it was heated with coal. One night while she was loading the stove it gave way and exploded, drenching the woman in flames. The blaze claimed the house as she ran out of it on fire. Running down the hollow, she was screaming an excruciating wail. She perished with the flames clinging to her body.

The legend that is told, states to this day and age that on various evenings a terrible scream can be heard, a scream that goes into the soul almost like the wail of a banshee. It will make a person freeze in their tracks with terror and their hair stand on end. If they are lucky, they might see an apparition in the form of a woman running, still to this day trying to get the flames off of her. A few people have seen and heard this specter, some were non-believers, but when it was over, they soon became believers. They know that something bizarre has happened and they don't care to go back to hear the terrifying screams in the hollow.

A friend I went to college with told this story to me. I would like to see if this legend does indeed have a screaming hollow.

THE MAN IN BLUE
Eyewitness Account

One night while working at a nursing facility we had an unoccupied room; this room was the first room in the hall. We could hear things dropping everywhere in the back hall. The residents in this hall could not move without assistance. Nobody was around to make these noises; the only people who were there could not possibly make these kinds of sounds. Lights would come on and go out, even the water in the unoccupied room would start running, but no one was there to turn it on. Some of the aides got spooked by these happenings, but the thing that rattled them the most was the man in blue that they saw. Especially when he faded away into nothing right in front of them.

There was a lady passing away in another hall, we thought maybe it was her husband who had already passed on coming to take her with him. Maybe the things that happened were his way of showing he was irate because we had moved her, and he couldn't find her. When he had died, they were both in the same hall. There are other sightings of this apparition. When other residents told us of seeing the man in blue it usually meant it was someone's time to pass and he was there to take them to their final home.

LOCKED DOORS
Eyewitness Account

After my dad passed away, we would get locked inside the house where we lived, sometimes we would even get locked outside too. The eerie problem with this was the locks were broken and the door keys wouldn't even work. The doors would open when we would say "ok dad, open up" and they opened.

I have no windows in my hall and keep the bedroom and bathroom doors locked so the dog and kids will stay out of the rooms. After the passing of my mother, one night the hallway lit up just like someone turned the light on. It was more like a flashlight beam; it stayed in one spot. The night she passed away I saw three quick lights moving outside the window. My father who had been deceased for five years was also seen in the hallway.

One afternoon when I came home from work to find my dog sitting in the locked bedroom in a corner, his hair standing straight up and scared to death. The lock on the door was locked; how the dog got in this bedroom we don't know. No one was at the house that week except me. The dog would not let anyone enter this room for several weeks. He went to great lengths to keep us out of the room. Sometimes we would lose our salt and pepper shakers only to find them in the microwave oven. We have also seen a ghostly image of a woman walking in the kitchen.

Final Goodbye
Eyewitness Account

During World War II my cousin was a crewmember on a bomber. They started out on a mission over Germany, but something happened on the plane, that caused it to catch fire. It crashed into a barn somewhere in England, my cousin perished in that crash. News traveled a little slower in those days. The Red Cross told us the news of his crash a few days later. What was strange about all of this is the night before we found out about the crash an eerie experience happened in my house. Something was pulling my hair as I was lying in bed, it held me down and I couldn't move. This happened for quite a long time on that night. I wasn't scared it was too bizarre to be scared. The same night at my uncle's house about a mile out the road, he heard someone pacing back and forth in his house. When he tried to get up, something pulled his hair holding him down – just like what had happened to me. We discussed this with each other the next day and didn't know what to think. The next day when the Red Cross told us about the crash, we knew then it was my cousin saying his final goodbye to us.

LOOKING ON

When I was a kid riding the school bus, it took us to this big old house where the bus turned around. My best friend and I always looked at this house because there was an old woman dressed in a dark orange coat staring out the window watching us.

What was weird about this was we saw her about every other day just staring out the same window, she was never outside. When I was almost out of high school my father and I passed this house on an afternoon drive. I told him about seeing the woman always staring out  the window watching the bus turn around. He told me that was impossible because no one had lived there in years and the woman that had lived there died about thirty years ago. He also told me she had worn a dark orange jacket most of the time. This was not the only time I had an experience at this house. After I grew up one of my friends was telling me of this haunted house out in the country, he had told of seeing apparitions there. I made him drive me to this house. When we pulled up to the driveway, it was the same house that the old woman in the dark orange coat looking on as our school bus was turning around all those years ago.

HAPPENINGS
Eyewitness Account

Many "eerie" things have happened since moving here to the old farm place, but we are not scared or frightened.

There was a box of my husband's old toys sitting in the hallway. One of the toys was an old metal train. It started making noises. Why was this strange? There were no batteries in it!

One evening while watching a show about applying make-up, I heard a phone ringing. "Our" phone was not ringing and there wasn't anything to do with a phone on the program.

While sitting on our porch we have heard voices coming from inside the house. The television, stereo, radio, and computer were not on. The voices are just audible enough to hear, but we are unable to make out the words or what's being said.

A hat my husband used to wear, has hung in our bedroom for about 3 years. One morning when I went into the bedroom the hat was lying in the middle of the floor.

Our dog will sometimes bark fiercely at the walls in the hallway and on occasion it sounds like someone is walking down the wall. We have never seen anything for the dog to bark at or anyone coming down the hall.

ROLLING ON
Eyewitness Account

There is a cemetery that sits upon a hill located in Ames Township. One evening back during the 1920's as the sun was setting and the moon rising, my uncle was on his way home in his buggy going past this cemetery.

When all of a sudden something unexpected appeared; it was all black and it rolled down the bank and in front of the horses. My uncle said it seemed to appear in the form of a body. It disappeared as suddenly as it appeared. The experience scared him so bad he cracked the whip on the horses and ran them as hard and fast as he could all the way home. He had traversed this road many times and had never seen anything like it ever again. After this ghostly sighting he was very cautious about traveling by this cemetery in the twilight hours.

PHONE CALL FROM BEYOND

In the 1970's my grandfather passed away. We were very close, he took me fishing and did most of the thing's grandparents do. He even taught me how to get on my grandmother's nerves. We were the best of buddies. My grandparents were married for more than 40 years. About a year after his passing I was visiting my grandma when the phone rang. I answered and got the shock of my life, the voice on the phone sounded exactly like my grandfathers. He asked if he could speak to my grandmother, she talked for a few minutes. I asked if that was grandpa calling, she never answered me. Till the day she passed away I never found out who exactly was on the phone that afternoon. Because of the expression on her face I always suspected it was grandpa calling from beyond to see how she was getting along.

GUEST ENTITY

While in bed one night I heard heavy footsteps walk thru the living room and down the hall to my bedroom. I felt a pressure on the opposite side of the bed. It was like someone sitting down. I thought maybe it was my dog. I listened to her breathing…. she was on my side of the bed on the floor. The entity then lay down on the other side of the bed. I put my arm out to see who or what was there. I felt nothing but the pressure that was on the mattress. It did not leave so I rolled over and went to sleep. It was weird because it never scared me. Nothing like it has happened since. My guest entity has never returned for a nap.

A NIGHT TO REMEMBER
Eyewitness Account

I've never experienced anything in my life like the tale I am about to relate. It was a Halloween night in 1996 when I was asked to participate in a séance. I had reservations (I always have reservations). At that time I lived in the Ironton, Ohio area, and for kicks I thought it would be a fun way to spook my girlfriend, who fully believed in such things and I was (at the time) a skeptic.

We arrived in an open field around 11 O'clock PM. There were 13 of us. I sat next to my girlfriend who was fully expecting to see something, but several of the friends with us told me that it was just a game. I agreed and sat with the group in the circle around a small campfire. The night was unseasonably warm and none of us wore coats. We all joined hands. The man presiding over the event (who I will call Jon), began to speak in all kinds of gibberish. I chuckled slightly and was shot a sharp look from him. I went silent and waited for all the magic to begin, but I still smiled widely for I was far from believing any of this.

It was about ten minutes into the gathering when things started to become slightly weird. Jon started to claim that he was someone else, a person named Six. Even Jon's voice started to change without any effort on his part. He began to make jokes at the expense of the group, upsetting some of the females with his rude remarks. When I protested, I began to find myself unable to speak, as if I were choking, with a lump in my throat. Then, like it started it stopped. Jon, (in the strange voice) told me that was only a taste of his power. Then as if he wished to be observed some more, several of the members in the group started to feel (as they told me later) sexually aroused.

Eric, who was the youngest in the group, decided he had, had enough and released my hand, breaking the chain. In one last defiance, the voice laughed, and the small camp-fire shot up in the air with a dynamic force. Jon fell back, he was breathing hard and he continued to say over and over, "Where was I?"

The night's events ended around twenty minutes after they had started. The group didn't stay around to chat about what happened. In fact, to this day some of them denied the thing ever took place. And some (my ex-girl-friend included) refuses to talk about it. Then there's me, I still have my doubts.
It's funny, but sometimes, at night I feel a lump in my throat and the warmth of the campfire.

DARK NIGHT
Eyewitness Account

Wind and rain blew hard across Athens County; it was eleven days before Christmas. Electric lines went down all over Athens. We were without electricity all afternoon and night. We borrowed a kerosene heater, gathered up our blankets and pillows, hugging the heater, then we settled down in the living room for a cold night's sleep. Just before dozing off, my husband turned off the heater and blew out the candles. I lay awake for a while and waited on the cold nights chill to come back in the house and wondered if the electric might come back on and what lights or appliances might come on with it. It was very dark inside the house as well as outside; there was no moon to give light on this night. I saw a circle blue in color about five inches in diameter, floating around in front of the entertainment center and our main front door. It just floated between these two places. I kept watching and looking to see what it might be...a reflection, or a light outside. There were no cars or lights outside, but like I said before it was very dark inside and out. I watched this blue orb a few minutes, and then dozed off to sleep. The next morning, I called my daughter to tell her of the sighting I had seen. She said when she had lived here with us, she had on occasion seen a red orb in the same vicinity. Was this someone or something watching over us in our cold nights sleep?

UNSOLVED MYSTERY OR LEGEND
Eyewitness Account

When I was a kid, I remember a half memory dream, I was at the babysitter's house near the West State Cemetery. I remember seeing a woman with a baby in her arms, it looked like it was bloody, running across the yard. I was four years old at the time, but the memory of the woman running with the child was etched in my mind for years. After moving back to Athens 25 years later,

I was giving my girlfriend a tour of the town. We went to the West State Cemetery, as I was telling her about this occurrence, we came  across the seven tombstones of a woman and her six children. All the children had died before the age of two.

None of them were dated at the same time, which I thought was weird. It wasn't like they all died in one big disaster the dates were all at different times. The eeriest thing was the tombstones were all dated in the early 1800's. So, after all those years of thinking about that woman running with the baby in her arms, I finally realized it was her ghost that I had seen at a young age. Could this be yet another unsolved mystery, we will never truly know. The answer to that is buried at the West State Cemetery.

DEATH PREMONITIONS
Eyewitness Account

I have been given several accounts of premonitions of upcoming death. It seems to happen in less than a month after the experience. I have heard these premonitions called tokens, omens, or death premonitions. This is an account of them. Are these visions real? The individuals who have experienced them believe they are. Here are a few experiences. The people who lived them want to remain anonymous.

One instance was when my grandmother passed away. My girlfriend saw my dad's green car stuck in the median strip on the highway. She never knew why this type of vision appeared to her until a few weeks later. My father was bringing my grandmother home one morning and she had a heart attack. He turned the car across the median strip and got stuck in the grass. His car was light green. Help arrived to take her to the hospital, but the heart attack was too much, and she died.

Another premonition that was told to me was about a sound of someone falling off of a chair or sofa so loud it woke the individual up. He ran out into the living room to see what was going on. There was no one in the house. About two weeks later one of his relatives was consumed in a fire in the living room of their house.

I was told that a woman who saw a ghostly apparition standing over her husband's favorite chair. The phantom had its head down in a state of mourning. She took a closer look revealing it was his favorite nephew. About two weeks later her husband passed away.

I was nine years old when my grandfather passed away. I was really upset, as we were very close. Just after I was told that he had passed away, I saw a vision of Jesus standing in our entryway.

The night before my Aunt died there were doors slamming and someone walking back and forth upstairs. This continued all night long. No one was upstairs, I checked. The next night she died.

When I was a young kid my mother was sick in the hospital with cancer. My father and I were in the bedroom one night when a bright light or star appeared in the window. It stayed for a few moments then it rose up into the sky and disappeared. The next morning my mother passed away.

THE DAY DAD DIED
Eyewitness Account

It was Friday morning, October 8, 1965. The two older girls (age 8 and 6) had just left for school; the two boys (age 4 and 1) were getting ready for breakfast. The baby girl, just 6 months old was still sleeping. It should have been a normal day, but for some strange reason, I felt an urgency to get the housework done early. We had a very big dining room, with four active kids and two dogs, and with the entrance into the house coming into that room; the linoleum floor was always a mess. But I felt a need to get that room cleaned and mopped early . . . it was like I had a deadline to meet. Anyone who knows me would know that was totally out of character, as I would figure "if it doesn't get done today, there's always tomorrow." Well, I fed the boys, got them dressed and had them help clean as best they could . . . picking up things, putting things away, and even dusting the furniture. Everything was going on like clockworks, no hassles, absolutely no problems. While the floor was drying, I got the baby up, fed and dressed her, and then finally put things back in place in the dining room, living room, kitchen, and bedrooms.

Just as I had finished, around 9:30 a.m., I saw my mother's car coming down the driveway, she wasn't driving, but the lady she picked up for work was driving. She should be at work, I thought, then I knew I had to go meet her at the door because at that moment I knew my dad had died and she would need comforted. As I got to the door, she said, "I wanted to stop here on my way home to tell you dad died."

My reply, "Yes, I know." (We didn't have a telephone and my husband was at work.) "I've got the kids ready, if you will take me on the hill to my in-laws, I'll call my husband and tell him so he can come home." We got into the car, went on the hill, and I called him. My younger sister was in high school and mom needed to go to her. She took me and the kids back home and I told mom we would be up as soon as my husband got home. She left. It was so strange; we didn't cry but just conducted the business at hand as calm and "common" as going to the grocery store. When my husband got home, we went to school to pick up the two girls, and then went to moms. Dad was only 56 years old; he had gone to a neighbor's house after mom had left for work and my sister had gone to school, just a friendly neighbor-visit. He was standing in the neighbor's kitchen, leaning against the doorway, talking. Suddenly he said he didn't feel too good and fell over. He died instantly. We later found out his heart had just quit; he'd had a massive coronary occlusion. He hadn't been sick, only complained of the usual muscle aches and pains from farming, so his death should have been shocking news. But I knew early that Friday morning that I was going to have a busy weekend and needed to get my housework done.

October 6, the Wednesday morning before, Dad had stopped by for a short visit; we had coffee and talked for a while. When he left, I knew that was the last time he would visit me. I remember thinking, "How morbid, how could I even think such a thing." I didn't mention my feelings to anyone, but on Friday morning, I knew even before mom got there.

MYSTERY WOMAN

We arose early one Saturday morning to go to Lancaster. On the way we stopped at a little cemetery in Haydenville. Up the narrow dirt road we drove. The morning mist was thick. Once we got to the cemetery the sun was trying to peek through the trees and the mist. The tombstones were old in this place. We had heard rumors of this cemetery being haunted, so we had to see if it was true. We took a few photos and were off on our shopping spree.

Upon returning home, we looked the pictures over and found something weird. In this photo there appeared to be a woman wearing a hat standing over in the corner

of the cemetery; she appeared to watch us. Was she just watching or was she guarding the cemetery? We will never know.
But the irony of this event is we lost the photo. Was it meant to be this way? Did we take a photo of something that wasn't supposed to be seen?

LAST LAUGH
Eyewitness Account

Sometime during the early 1960's there was a man that I had as an employee. He was poor, and he did not mind doing things that were unlawful to get money. That came to an end in one night. The guy's name was Dave. One-night Dave stopped by my house to tell me this story. He and his brother were out driving around when they found an abandoned house. The people that had lived in it died a few years before this happened. Needing some extra money, they decided to see if there was anything in this house worth taking. Dave said they tried to break in, but they couldn't get the door to open. Not getting in through the door they pried open a window and went in. They rummaged around for a little bit and found an old sewing machine. Deciding they could get a few bucks for it they started to take it out the window. All of a sudden, they heard two people laughing. They started looking for someone else in the house. They couldn't find anyone in the house, but the laughing continued. Dave said it put the fear of death in them, as the laughing got louder. They jumped out of the window and got away from this house as fast as they could. They did not get the sewing machine, but Dave did say that the old folks that lived there got the last laugh. As far as I know he nor his brother ever went past that house again.

DEAD MAN'S WALK

When I was a young child, I was sitting on the couch watching the television. My dad and mom were outside in the yard. It was just starting to turn dark. While watching the TV I heard someone walking toward the living room. I couldn't see anyone. I leaned forward on the couch and there it was, a pair of dress shoes sliding across our hard wood floor. They were moving by themselves. This scared me so bad all I could do was watch them slide right past me. I did wonder if this was really happening or did, I imagine it. When my parents came in the house, they asked me why the pair of dress shoes was in the middle of the kitchen floor? I think they thought I put them there. But I watched the ghost of a dead person walk in the kitchen with them.

WATCHFUL EYE
An Eyewitness Account

After returning from a late evening shopping trip that my daughter and I went on, we got a phone call. It was her uncle Bill, as she happened to be the one who answered it. It really upset her he had called to warn us of an escaped criminal who jumped from a train in our town. This man was rumored to be very dangerous and wanted for many crimes. I took our dog out for a walk in our back yard. There was a figure standing by the clothesline. At first, I thought this was the man we were warned about. It really put a cold chill up my spine. I thought maybe we were not going to make it through the night. Upon a closer look this figure appeared to a female dressed in black. Her dress looked to be something that was worn it the 1930's. I turned around and went back in the house. I called my husband to tell him and he told me that this was his Aunt just watching over everyone. This is not the first time she had appeared in a time of stress. So, was she watching for the escaped man? Or was she keeping a watchful eye on us?

WALKING ANGEL
Eyewitness Account

On a bright moonlit night my Uncle Frank was walking home by himself; he did this quite often as he only lived a mile from my house. On his way home on that evening he looked off the road into the meadow. There was a woman walking in the field. Frank never thought too much about it until he got closer to her.

He didn't know what to think when he saw what she looked like; she was dressed in white he later told me. The thing that was eerie was she had wings on her back. He had never seen anything like this in his life. She walked for a while then disappeared. My uncle believed this to be an angel walking him home. He often spoke of this phenomenon but never seen her again.

STANDING IN THE DOOR

One morning about 3:00 am I woke to find a woman standing in my bedroom door. She was dressed in white and was translucent.

Being able to see through her made me think, "This is a dream". I pulled the pillow over my head for a few minutes then I looked again, she was still there. I could not make out a face to see who it was. I looked at my dog lying on the foot of the bed, she was also watching this woman standing in the doorway. What really got me thinking was the dog always starts barking when someone strange is in the house, but the dog was wagging its  tail. This went on for about ten minutes then the woman faded into nothing. So far, she has never reappeared again. I was later talking to my landlord and he said a woman had died a few years ago and she stayed here. Was she looking back on her place to see who lived here now?

PASSING THROUGH

Late one night while sleeping on the sofa I awoke as a figure passed by me and went into the kitchen. This apparition appeared to be female with a long blue nightgown. It walked right into the kitchen.

Thinking it was my wife I yelled for her. I got a big surprise when she answered, and she was in the bedroom. This made me really wonder who it was. Thinking maybe we had an intruder I jumped up and ran into the kitchen. There was nothing there. My wife came out to the living room to see what I was making such a fuss about. I told her what had happened, she said maybe it was just a ghost passing through. This happened some time ago but still to this day I often think about the woman in the blue gown. Was this really her spirit just passing through? Or does she reside in our home and this was her first appearance. She hasn't been spotted since, but I don't think I want to look for her.

THE BOILING CAULDRON
Eyewitness Account

Back in the mid 1800's a professor needed a skeleton for the bone structure. He obtained a body, how no one knows for sure. This professor cut the body up into pieces and placed it in a big iron cauldron filled with water. He built an enormous fire under the kettle and brought it to a boil.

The body was boiled until all that was left was the bones of an unknown man. In that day and age this kind of cruel travesty must have been commonplace. This iron cauldron was located out in the woods close to Athens. Not too long after this occurred, on certain rainy nights a person could see a light in the section of woods where this took place. Was this a light of the fire or the spirit of the nameless man trapped in the location where his body was desecrated? No one can answer that question. Even now more than a hundred years later the light can be seen on certain rainy nights.

ARROWS OF FIRE
Eyewitness Account

This is a strange story that happened late one night while Jim and I were out coon hunting. The dogs were way ahead of us, they had a coon treed; we started across a flat in the woods. As we were walking, the sky lit up with fire. This was spooky it was arrows with fire on them. The arrows landed about ten feet in front of us. The next odd thing that happened was the arrows and the flames disappeared,

without leaving a trace of ever being there. I had never seen anything like that before. After being scared half to death, we gave up on coon hunting for that night. I did get enough nerve to go back a few days later. There was no sign of any fire. The only thing I did see was an odd pile of stones about a hundred yards from where we were standing. I think maybe we were coming upon some kind of Indian burial site. Maybe that is why the arrows appeared, because the spirits did not want us to trespass, at least on this night anyway. The arrows of fire were the most mysterious thing that I have ever seen.

SLAMMING DOOR

It was a late summer night in the midnight hour. My wife and I were asleep in bed, when suddenly I heard a loud bang. This brought me out of a deep sleep and right out of the bed. Thinking we had an intruder I grabbed a ball bat and went searching through the house. There was nothing to be found, so I went back to bed. It happened again. My wife and I were kept up most of the night by this strange loud banging of a door. The next day we started inquiring into these strange phenomena. We found out from the previous tenants that it happened about once a year in the early summer. We had also discovered the woman who once owned the house had died in the room where the door slammed. We think she must have come back to check on her house.

The Touch
Eyewitness Account

After we had an exhausting day at work, my husband and I finally got to bed around midnight. About half hour to forty-five minutes of lying there and just dozing off into the twilight of sleep, I felt something rubbing the lower calf of my leg. I opened my eyes to see only my husband's back. There was no possible way that he could have done this. I woke him up and told him of what just happened. I turned a little and moved closer to him. A few minutes went by and I felt the same soft rubbing on my back. Again, I woke him and told him it was now rubbing my back. This was enough! I explained to my husband that I no longer felt comfortable sleeping in our bed. We moved into the living room to sleep the rest of the night. I then had a very peaceful night's sleep.

PHANTOM DRIVER
Eyewitness Account

This story happened in Toronto Ontario Canada and was passed on to be told here. In 1987 I lived at Morningside and Sheppard. I went to a bar at Military Trail and Morningside; I had one beer while waiting for my friend to show up. I phoned him to see where he was, he wasn't home. Anyway, I left the bar at Military Trail and Morningside to walk home. I was wearing jeans and a leather jacket as I was walking along Morningside (I forget the time of night) there is no cars and no other people anywhere. It was snowing pretty bad, and I was freezing. When I looked up, I seen a car coming towards me on the side of the road I was walking on. There wasn't any engine sound and the guy lowered his car window and yells "Hey you wanna a ride?" Now I don't like to get into strangers cars but I was cold so I climbed into a tan colored Datsun, the guy asked where I was going, I said I'm going to the next set of lights which is Morningside and Sheppard. We talked but I forgot about what. Anyway, we got to Morningside and Sheppard and I said" this is my stop". The guy stops the car I get out. I see no tire tracks from the direction we came from. I walked in front of the car to cross the road to the islands that separate the two lanes. I turn to look where the car was and the car wasn't there, there wasn't tire tracks going forward or u-turning. No car, no tracks nothing! But yet I was in a car and got out of a car. Where did the car go and where were the tire tracks? I never saw the car or the driver again. I'm not nuts or loony. Anyway, thought I'd share my story believe it or not it happened to me, I was there.

BURIED ALIVE
Eyewitness Account

One time quite a few years back, a couple friends and I took an afternoon and went bicycle riding. The scenery caught our eye around a place called Drakes, which isn't far from McLeish and Hartleyville. We got a little thirsty and hungry, so we stopped at a nearby filling station to get a snack to tide us over. We went back the same way curious as to what was up the fork of the road we'd seen earlier. We saw a few houses and a cemetery. The cemetery was Walnut Grove.

A story was told of an awful death of a lady that was buried alive in this cemetery. This was way back before embalming was even heard of, probably late 1700's or early 1800's. The story that was passed down through the generations was that the woman buried alive could still be heard from her grave in a muffled voice saying, "Help I am alive, I am alive". We stopped at the cemetery and started looking around. I walked away from my friends and found some bushes as I needed to relieve myself. I thought someone was behind me, so I turned around and asked if he was ready to go. There was no one there. I have to say I got out of there a lot faster than I went in!

THE COFFIN
Eyewitness Account

A story was told about a three-story brick building where a man was beheaded. In this same building I could see a casket in the window when I passed by. Every time I would pass this building the casket would

be in a different window. It was never in the same spot for very long. I would go by one week it would be on the first floor, maybe the next week it would be on the third floor. This building was condemned, and the doors were all blocked off. I always wondered if someone was moving this casket. If someone was moving it, they sure went to a lot of trouble moving it from the first floor to the third floor or the second floor or did the casket move on its own. Could the man that was beheaded be looking for his head?

GRANDMA'S HUTCH
Eyewitness Account

When I was younger and in elementary school my grandmother and I were very close. My grandmother always watched over me like most grandmas. She died when I was in the fifth grade. There was an old German Schrunk in the hallway that we kept things in; it had belonged to my grandmother.

One afternoon after coming home from school I wanted to write a letter to my friend. I went to the Schrunk to get my stationery; I dug through everything it wasn't anywhere to be found. I looked in the kitchen and living room too. Giving up on finding it, I went into the living room for something and on my way back to the kitchen, a white shadow reflected in the glass on the Schrunk. Not thinking too much about it at the time, I kept on going. As I entered the kitchen there my stationery was on a chair. Twenty years after to this day, I think my grandmother had found my missing stationery and set it where I could find it.

GLOWING LIGHT
Eyewitness Account

One evening about 9:30, there was a group of us sitting in the parking lot at Concord Church. I looked up toward the end of the cemetery and saw a glowing light. Then the other two people with me saw this light

before it flickered out. Sitting there dumbfounded, we thought maybe it was a car or house light, but no cars came by us. We immediately drove up where the light was seen. There was no way it was a house light. There wasn't anyone around but the three of us. It happened about 200 yards from where we were parked. I wondered if I had imagined it happening, but I had two witnesses. Over the years there have been rumors of this cemetery being haunted. We all wondered what the light was; maybe it was a ghost of the past checking on the cemetery.

This was taken at Concord cemetery.

STRANGER IN THE NIGHT

As a kid I used to hear family members talking about strange things that they had seen or that had occurred, that had spooked them. I myself had never really had too many things happen to me that I can remember. I don't know if I just wrote them off as being a sissy or maybe my imagination playing tricks on me. I never thought too much about it until my mom, stepdad and I moved to Scatter Ridge. That's when the weird things started happening.

The thing that happened to me to make me really believe was in the wee hours of the morning in the summer. (I was a sophomore in high school then I think.) I remember waking up and seeing a man dressed completely in black standing at the foot of my bed. I thought I was dreaming so I kept blinking my eyes, but I was actually very awake. My heart pounded with fear and all I could do was lie there. I couldn't roll over or even pull the covers over my head. This tall dark man had clothes like maybe an Amish person would wear. Not your everyday black Levi jeans and button-up shirt. His clothing looked like something that would have been worn back in the early days around the late 1800's to early 1900's. He was probably about 6' tall with a slim build and long straight hair. He wore a button up, black shirt and a long trench coat. But not like a trench coat you could buy now days, more like one that was worn back in the cowboy days. I could feel his eyes peering from underneath his hat. (I can't explain what kind of hat it was other than old and black.) His teeth were also rather scary. It was almost like they were pointed.

I still to this day don't understand why he was so mad at me. And I don't even know who or why he was there, but he just stood there for most of the night and glared at me. In the morning when I told my mom and stepfather what had happened, they as usual didn't act surprised that I had finally had a ghostly experience. I think when I was able to come to terms with what had happened to me, it was like I had opened myself up and had become more susceptible to happenings than anyone in the house.

THE OLD CABIN
Eyewitness Account

There is an old house in Ashland, Kentucky, around 100 years old. It's an old
log cabin, built on what some people
have always speculated was an old Indian burial ground. There is a slope
that falls over where the cabin is.
When we were younger, old Indian
arrowheads and other types of arti-
facts were found while we were playing. But, my mom
was always adamant that when you take something from
Indians, you were to put it back, because when she was
younger, she was in the house with her sister and a lot of
things happened to them. Her sister was strangled in the
bedroom; they were both 11 years old, they barely got to
her in time; she had little marks, like you would have
when being strangled or having strangulation on her
neck. My mother's sister used to sleep in what was
known as the "back room". One night, they were both
sleeping in the same bed, my mother got up to go to the
bathroom, and when she came back there was something
that had her sister Wanda by the neck, pushing her and
forcing her down on the bed. At first my mom thought it
was some kind of convulsion, but it wasn't. Other things
that happened in the house when my mother was young,
was blood flowing down the wall in one room; this scares
her to death today. Three people in the family have been
killed at that home at different times, and only a few
people would ever stay in the cabin. Since the cabin had
been built, you would have one circumstance after an-

other occur. But during the various times the cabin has been sitting there, there has been a fireball incident, two of those; my mother when she was a teenager saw it... as you're coming down one part of the highway, the house sits on a hill and you can see the whole hillside, and she saw a fireball, which I always considered to be a ball of lightening, but to her it was flames spinning, it covered over the house. The second time, it was seen by her sister Wanda, and she saw it hover over the roof, but didn't do any gyrating motions like a bolt of lightning might do, it didn't jump, it just hovered, one of her brothers was killed the next night. So, they thought it was a big kind of omen. Other things normal to hauntings, like lights flickering on and off... the kitchen was the worse place for that; pots and pans would bang, and of course, we have the front room that was constructed differently from the house, the walls and floor were made of concrete, it was naturally cool there when you walk in; you'd walk in and you could always feel it right behind you until you would get to the kitchen, the second part of the house. If you would stand there for a few minutes, you could feel or imagine someone tapping you, the wind on your hand, or your shoulder, but it wouldn't follow you into the kitchen, it stays right in that room, and that's where my uncle passed away.

THE CAR FROM NOWHERE
Eyewitness Account

In the mid 1980's I worked the late shift in Athens, Ohio and had to drive home early in the morning, just as the sun was coming up. What made the drive so annoying was at that time the bridge on State Route 550 just beyond Sugar Creek, was being replaced so I had to cut down Bean Hollow Road and over the ridge to get home. I had driven the road a lot and knew it well, so it was only a minor inconvenience. Early one morning I found myself being followed closely by another car. I had never encountered another car that early before, but it did not surprise me. The car was following too close and was bugging me. So, I hung over to the right to allow the car to pass.

As it did, I noticed the car was an older model from the 1940's. As it continued past, I took a glimpse at the driver; it was an older man. His appearance gave me cold chills up my spine. He was all white with a thin face that pointed out into a sharp nose. He didn't look over at me, so, I really couldn't see his eyes. The car pulled out in front of me and turned a curve as I followed. As I went around the curve, the old car was gone. It seemed to vanish. My heart skipped a beat and I raced quickly over the ridge to get back to 550. I've driven that road many times before and have never encountered the car again. But sometimes as I drive it at night my heart skips a beat when another car approaches me from behind.

THE LANTERN GUY
Eyewitness Account

There were numerous sightings of what I like to call the "lantern guy". My mom and my father told me it was my uncle, because when he was alive, he would do a routine every week; he was very adamant about going up to the graveyard, he'd leave the house every night about 10:00 at night and go up a slight hill, he'd take a lantern, put a floppy hat on and a raincoat, and check things out to make sure things were okay to him. That same figure has been seen numerous times; I have seen it myself, and just recently.

My older brother Kenneth and my mom, when he was in high school, saw it about 2:00 in the morning. It was raining pretty heavily and they saw what appeared to be a man walk down to the graveyard, down the road that led to the cabin, and walked to the front door. I have also seen this same figure, but different in deviation which kind of perplexes me; it was 3 or 3:30 in the morning, my dog barks at anything, well, he started barking and barking, and all of a sudden, he just shuts up. I stayed up late, and I just kind of peeked out to see what was going on, and there was a figure. The figure was standing in the wood pile. If you can imagine glaring at it, you would see it, but if you focused your eyes on it, you would realize it wasn't standing on the wood, just kind of sitting there. It stayed for a few minutes, and then walked to the cabin front door; I knew then I wasn't hallucinating that one. The next day, I told my mom and she went to see my uncle who said nobody had come in. It doesn't bother my uncle; it has never bothered him; my mother and father speculate that it is my deceased uncle doing his routine. He was very caring about the property, the trees, and if someone would cut down a tree, it would freak him out. He was very constant about keeping everything the way it is supposed to be. I think this could be him still checking the place over with his lantern.

MIDNIGHT MENACE
Eyewitness Account

A few weeks after moving in a small house in Athens County. One night while trying to sleep I heard footsteps walking in the hall of the upstairs. It just happens to be where my bedroom is located. There has been a window that opens on its own even when it is locked. One evening I heard a phone ringing which was really odd since I had no phone or even phone service. At first, I thought maybe it was the neighbors, but I realized with all the traffic and outside noise it couldn't be any of my neighbor's phones. The footsteps that I hear are possibly footfalls of a man it is a heavy walk. Every once in a while, I can feel a presence at the foot of my bed. There was even knocks on the wall above the headboard. This sure did make it a sleepless night. I haven't slept in the upstairs since that has happened. Every once in a while, I can see a face out of the corner of my eye it appears to be a face of a man. I am not sure if this house I live in is haunted, but some strange things has happened in it. One thing is for sure; I had a mischievous visitor in the midnight hours.

THE CARETAKER
Eyewitness Account

On the edge of Athens and Vinton County is where Bowen Cemetery is located. Legend is the figure of a man wearing a top hat and cape guards and roams the cemetery. This apparition has been seen in the cemetery several times over the years. There has been talk of supernatural activity going on there for a long time.

Not too long after we moved close to Bowen Cemetery, we could hear strange noises. After going outside to look there was never anyone there. We started to build a picket fence around our yard. After we went in for the evening, we could hear pounding like maybe someone was out in the yard working on the fence. To our surprise there was no one there when we looked outside. Another time after gathering some firewood we heard the pounding again I thought it was my nephew splitting the wood upon looking outside no one was to be seen. I also found out that he hadn't been home. To this day we still wonder what the noise was. Could this be the figure that guard's the cemetery pounding to let us know he was around? On a summer evening just before dark I was looking down the road at Bowen Cemetery. I saw a green tarp lying in the cemetery just like the ones grave diggers use to cover a fresh grave with. Figuring there was going to be a funeral the next day we went over to the graveyard to see who was going to be buried. To our surprise there was no tarp or fresh grave. Could this have been the spectral caretaker playing around with us or maybe it was a warning of a death soon to be.

HAUNTED HOUSE
Eyewitness Account

The two-story house that I reside in was built on or by a cemetery. I can look out my window and see what looks like an old tombstone; there is no writing on it. That is all that seems to be marked, the rest of the graves are in my side yard.

The cemetery does show up on topographical maps. I live in one of two houses that are side by side. Since I have lived there, people have told me of the eerie stuff that went on at the house. One story I had heard was from a visitor that was sleeping on the sofa. He woke up around three in the morning and watched the spectral figure of a woman dressed in white walking through the living room. She disappeared by the front door. The aspect of my house being haunted was intriguing to me. So, one night I got out the Ouija board.

(The Ouija board is a board with the alphabet and numbers and a pointer used for various forms of divination and/or spirit contact. It is not recommended to use one of these as it could bring worse trouble than a person already has,) I asked for the spirit that walked through the living room to talk to me. I got the name of Sue. She was a little girl who haunts the house. She plays on the steps and in the kitchen. A friend of mine came to visit he is somewhat in tune with the supernatural. He told me there were a few spirits in the house and on the property. The one he sensed inside was that of a female and that she plays on the steps. Late at night I have heard tapping on my window and people walking around upstairs. I hear the noises when there is no one else home. My roommate has heard the tapping as well. There is a lot of noise in the upstairs. A friend stayed one night, she woke up, she couldn't move, she felt like she was being held down in bed. She said it was almost like something was trying to enter her body. She also felt like someone was sitting on her chest. After the stuff I have written here, I wonder if the people buried in the cemetery haunt our house because no one remembers them. Could the little girl on the stairs be playing to get our attention so she won't be forgotten?

GHOST RIDER
Eyewitness Account

When I lived in Kentucky in the early 1990's I remember a time that I had looked into the past. A friend of mine lived out in Boyd County, several miles outside of Ashland. We had just finished dinner and we stepped out behind his house so he could smoke, because his wife wouldn't let him smoke inside. Our conversation was far from what we were about to encounter. As we talked, we heard hoof beats coming from a group of trees at the far end of a field that was behind his home.

We stopped talking and watched. From the trees came a rider dressed in a Union uniform, he had a sword pulled out and pointed in front of him as he rode in a battle position. My friend yelled out to him, but the rider acted as if he didn't hear his shouts. The rider was about a half a football field away from us, so we  couldn't get a clear look at his face. Seconds later the horse returned to another crop of trees and disappeared as if he had never been there. We stood silent for a time and then began to discuss what it could have been. We surmised it could have been a part of a civil war reenactment, but neither of us knew of any such thing around at the time. We were both amazed and when we told my

friend's wife, she laughed at us and told us to stop drink-
ing, (which we were not doing.) In any case we knew what
we saw, whether it was true or not, it makes a good story.

NIGHT PROWLERS
Eyewitness Account

Out in the hills around Nelsonville, Ohio there is a cemetery named Pedigo; it is said to be haunted. One night a buddy and I were out running the back roads looking for something to do. We decided to go past this cemetery thinking maybe we might see a spook or something. We stopped by it for a few minutes. We saw no ghosts or anything else in the cemetery. Thinking it was just another legend we decided to move on. It was about three in the morning and we were less than a half a mile from the cemetery, when we saw a big woman hunched over walking. There was also a man walking along beside her. They took no notice of us driving by. They didn't even look up, it was like they didn't even see us. They were dressed in clothes that people wore about a hundred years ago. I wondered if we imagined this. We sped up and got away from there. To this day I don't know if they were apparitions or real. Walking up a gravel road at three in the morning is odd enough anyway. I still see their images in my mind to this day. It was a weird experience. If they we specters, then maybe they were on their way back to the cemetery after their late-night prowl.

DEAD OF NIGHT
Eyewitness Account

After coming home from having surgery on my shoulder I was almost dependent on my husband. All I was able to do was sit in a chair. I was in my chair when my husband went to bed, I tried to sleep, but the pain was horrible. I would doze off to sleep then I would be awake. Late in the night after everything had settled down, I heard someone coming up the hall. I thought my husband had decided to sleep on the couch. I heard the sofa weigh down like someone laying on it. They even tossed around a little, but no one was on the couch. Sitting in the chair made it even worse because I was helpless to even move. I was petrified from fear. I never seen anyone or anything on the sofa. I told him about it the next morning. I was thinking that if my blankets would have move, I would have screamed.

THE LETTER
Eyewitness Account

I used to live in a house a few miles outside the town of Rutland, Ohio. Our furnace would make a noise that sounded like footsteps going through the house. Even at times when the furnace wasn't on, we would still hear footsteps going through our house. After about a year and a half of listening to it and not figuring out what it was, my mom got a letter in the mail. It was from a preacher. My mom had never had any contact with this preacher, she had never even heard of him before. She showed me the letter that said, "we were in God's hands and everything would be alright". I guess the weird thing is that the footsteps stopped after we received the letter.

COMING HOME
Eyewitness Account

My great-grand-father's home was on Sand Ridge road, and after all the years it is still there. He had one leg off; so, he would ride his buggy right up to the house. After he passed from this world, it was told that you still can hear him come up the driveway with his horse and buggy. It will stop about to the back door and he would get out, then the horse will go on to the barn. As far as I know this can still be heard at the old house. I had a girlfriend that lived there when we were growing up; I spent lots of nights with her in that house. We heard strange noises but never could explain them to anyone. Was this my great-grand-father walking through the house with his one good leg after letting his horse and buggy go to the barn?

PHANTOM WALKER
Eyewitness Account

When I was a teenager the house we lived in; we could hear like a woman in high heel shoes walking around. No one had ever seen anything or anyone. This happened every once in a while. One evening I remember my two brothers heard her upstairs, and one ran upstairs while the other yelled up to him which room he could hear her in, but nothing was ever seen. We would hear her come down the stairs but when you opened the door at the bottom of the steps nothing was there.

GHOST HOUND

When I was a young kid about six years old; my mother was sick. She stayed in the bedroom at our house and my dad and I slept on the couch that folded into a bed. One night I awoke to see this dog in our house. It walked up to the couch and turned its head over on the pillow. It seemed very playful; I was sitting up when this happened. What made this experience interesting was the fact that we had no dog. Even if we would have it would not have been a house dog. After a couple of minutes, it turned to walk away, and then it just disappeared. I often thought that I imagined the dog. Maybe it really happened I guess I will never know if the hound was a specter wanting petted or just a child's imagination in the late-night hours.

CRY BABY BRIDGE OF ZALESKI

Traveling through Zaleski State Forest on the way to the Moonville Tunnel there is a metal bridge that spans Raccoon Creek. The bridge is about a quarter of a mile from the tunnel. I was recently told of a legend about this bridge. And of a woman who didn't want her newborn baby. So, she climbed down to the creek, walked under the bridge and threw the child in the water drowning it. The legend goes that at midnight of a waxing moon if a person stops their car in the middle of the bridge and lays the keys on the hood of their vehicle. They will hear a baby cry. There are a lot of similar ghost stories about cry baby bridges like this one. A few of them are told throughout the state of Ohio. This one just seems to add a little more to the Moonville legend. Along with the ghost in the tunnel, the old cemetery and other ghost sightings in the area. Did a baby drown under the bridge? Is this just a folklore tale to scare people? There is only one way to know for sure; go to the bridge at midnight stop your vehicle and lay the keys on the hood. If you dare to tempt the fates. I have never tried it yet. So, the question remains is the story of the bridge true? It is for you the reader to decide.

LOOKING FOR GRANDMA

In Athens County there is an old farmhouse that seems to have a history of its own. For in its front yard sits an Indian mound. There have been reports of strange happenings in this house, one of which was written as "A Picture of Grandma". We had the opportunity to visit this house one evening. There were four of us in our group armed with flashlights and cameras. We had hoped the spirits were still in this house. We entered with a lot of skepticism of seeing anything out of the ordinary. We took several photos and seen nothing, when suddenly boards started creaking on the stairs. That sure did get every one's attention. Then our cameras started to have some kind of mechanical problems like batteries dying or film messing up. Flashlight batteries started to die. Once we got everything going again, we started taking more photos. Seeing things in other rooms was quite common the longer we stayed. It seemed we had stirred something from its rest. We made our way to the upstairs to a room as long as the house. The long room it was named. As I walked in this long room, I had an eerie feeling almost like a freezing cold gust of wind. It was a feeling of dread and I wondered if we were supposed to be here. It seemed like we were followed throughout the house. After getting out of this room and back downstairs we went outside and heard something come crashing around a building.

Everyone froze to see what this was. It was only a dog that got loose. I wonder if we were welcome in the house. When we got home to view the pictures, we had taken we found all kinds of weird things from orbs to something that looked like a skull.

THE GHOST OF THE TOWER

It was sometime in the late 1980's when I was working in Cutler Hall on the campus of Ohio University. I remember one evening after everyone left for the night., things were not so quite on the third floor. While doing my tasks I looked up and seen a ghostly figure standing in the hallway. Dismissing it as my imagination, I proceeded with my work. As I was leaving the room, I heard a voice whisper. I couldn't make out what it was saying. Another incident happened one evening when I was in the stairwell on the third floor and something tapped me on the shoulder. The only thing I was thinking about was to get the hell out of here. The next few weeks similar occurrences happened. It was right after these events I started doing some research on Cutler Hall.

This is what I was able to find through various articles and stories. Cutler Hall was built in 1819 and is one of the oldest buildings on campus. There is an old story that someone had

died in the clock tower. There have been reported sightings of a figure in the tower. Not much else has been written about the haunting in Cutler Hall.

Was my experience a manifestation from the ghost of the tower? Or was it a late evening imagination running wild? These questions may never be answered. The one sure fact is I was glad that I never had to go back there when the building was empty.

THE GHOST HUNT AT HOLLISTER

It was a cold January evening when we traveled to the Hollister Cemetery. There were three of us on this evening and we all had hopes of seeing an apparition. We wandered through the graveyard taking photos and looking. It was very cold on this night. In our whole hour there we saw nothing out of the ordinary. Only when we started towards the car did something start to make a crashing sound in the bushes right beside of us. It had startled Amanda and Chuck for a minute. Then some birds came crashing out.

This was the only weird thing that had happened, until we got our film developed. There were several unexplainable things in the pictures. This mist appeared in this photo but not in the one after it. We had several photos with orbs in them. One of the photos had a strange wavy light in it, which was eerie since it was taken in total darkness. A large orb appeared in this photo; it seemed to have an inside that was different colors. Being very skeptical about these photos no one could explain since the anomalies appeared on the nega- tives too. I have often wondered if the spirits were letting us know they were willing to be seen on that night.

THE OLD BARN

In Athens County just off a two-lane road is an old farm, the house is long gone. An outbuilding is all that is left of this farm. One fall afternoon while out doing research for a project we came to this building. After going in it we climbed to the upper room. This upper room seemed kind of eerie. It also seemed like a good place for kids to play in. There was a deck of cards lying on the floor like maybe someone else had found this hideout before. We took a few pictures of the inside of this building.

Orbs started showing up in some of the photos. We never started out on a ghost hunt, but it just happened to be what it was. Most of the time people look for ghosts at night but this was around 1:30 in the afternoon. There were three of us in this outing. Nici kept talking about how she felt like children were in this upstairs room playing. Upon leaving we came upon an old family cemetery. There were five graves in it; two of them were children who died at a young age in the late 1800's. I often

wonder if Nici was right in her feelings of children playing in that room. Maybe they never left the farm they had
lived on in the past and were still playing every day. I do
know that we got a little more than we expected on that
day.

Creatures and UFO's

A VISITATION OF THE SHADOW PEOPLE
Eyewitness Account

What are shadow people? Elusive creatures that hide in the dark places; there is little evidence that these beings exist, besides the occasional glimpse out of the corner of your vision. It is said they are translucent but can become solid when they truly want to frighten a person and usually appear to be around ten feet tall.

What is known about these shadows is more conjecture then fact. As stated before, these shadow creatures are best seen from the corner of your vision. Quick glimpses, as you read a book, or watch T.V. Some people claim to spot them riding in the car in the passenger seat as they drive. Most cases of shadow people are reported inside, but there is the odd encounter with them outdoors, resting against trunks of trees, or their shining eyes peering from tall grass where they hide. Inside encounters involve mirrors, closets and yes even underneath the bed.

When I was five years old, I lived in Columbus, Ohio. I remember many dreadful nights wondering what lurked beneath my bed or hid in the closet of my bedroom, that had that ominous aura about it, there wasn't a night that I didn't sleep in a fetal possession under my covers, daring not to peek out. Then there are the solid encounters, seeing them across a dark hall, or standing on a flight of stairs.

I remember my brother claiming to see someone entering our parents' bedroom late one night when I was quite young, he of course dismissed it as our father coming home from the late shift; but my mom informed him dad had not come home yet. Back then we called it a ghost, now I'm not so certain. Have you ever heard someone call your name and there would be no one in the room with you? Shadow people are far from silent. If you are subject to this, a shadow person might have contacted you, so next time stop and look around and don't dismiss those sounds so easily.

Cold chills are often common with high anxiety, fear, or revelations. But an unseen presence can also be the cause of this feeling. Have you ever turned on all the lights in the house? Then turned on the stereo so you won't feel so alone. Maybe you were feeling the prying eyes of what you could not see or perhaps you have had an encounter with a shadow person. Don't be frightened, there could be many other reasons you've felt this way, but if you have thought it through and there are no other reasons a shadow person may be the cause after all.

Bumps in the night could be another encounter with the shadow people. Footsteps, creeks in the floorboards, even objects such as pictures on the wall, or pots sliding off the countertop could be caused with a brush from a shadow person. Then there are those odd sounds you hear when you lie in bed, when you are just between awake and sleep; should you get up and check? Next time you may reconsider that and let the unknown be. Not convinced? Then you are not alone.

As I said before there is little evidence that points to the fact shadow people are nothing more than our minds playing tricks with our perceptions. But if they are real, what do they want? Are they studying us? If that's the fact, then perhaps they have discovered that it has been reversed on them and now we are the researchers. Perhaps they are aliens? Or they have come to us from another dimension. Have they slipped sideways in time? The speculation is endless, reaching towards stupidity. Still, this doesn't diminish the fact that there are people who have come to believe that shadow people are real, despite the verification of their identity. It is their undeniable faith which will most certainty bring the shadow people into the light, but for now skepticism wins the debate. But you have to wonder right now, are you being watched?

WATCHING BIGFOOT
Eyewitness Account

Bigfoot is a crypto zoological creature that has been spotted all over the United States for years. A lot of research has gone into finding Bigfoot. Sightings and witnesses are numerous. There are several organizations devoted to studying the Bigfoot phenomena. This is an account of a sight that happened in Athens County.

Search on for Big Foot

Not too far from Athens, back in the early 1970's I was going out to get my laundry off the clothesline. I just happened to look up in the meadow. There was something walking across the grass. As I got a closer look it had hair all over its body and stood upright. I wondered to myself... is this a bear? If it was a bear it would have to be a grizzly cause this creature was big. I hid around the corner of our building and watched this creature with curiosity. This beast had a funny walk. Could this be an escaped gorilla?

Then I realized this was a Bigfoot. As I watched it disappear into the woods, I wished I could have thought to get my camera to take a picture.

For me the image will forever be etched in my memory.

THE BLACK PANTHER
Eyewitness Account

Back in the 1960's our old family farmhouse burnt down. Around 1972 I finally decided to remove the remains of the house. It was a warm day when I started this project. I dropped the blade on the dozer to push the house down. For some reason I decided to stop so my son and I could have a look under the house. We looked the sandstone foundation over and saw nothing, so I proceeded to push the house off its foundation. Suddenly, some big black creature jumped out onto the hood of the dozer.

It had a long tail and resembled a giant cat. It was on the hood of the dozer and we were face to face and eye to eye, I didn't know what to do. So, this creature and I just stared each other down for a few minutes. Then it jumped off the hood and walked over the hill with grace like nothing was going to bother it. As it was disappearing into the woods, I realized I had just stared down a black panther. This was not the end of this creature; it was spotted in the meadows by people passing by. Then a few weeks later a friend that lived about 2 miles from my place was telling me he had seen a black panther. It was standing in the middle of the road in front of his house. He said the moon was full and moonlight really made this cat look neat. But the other twist was when he was watching it another one stepped into the road too. This thing was spotted occasionally, for a few years. When houses started to be built on this ridge it has disappeared. But it will not to be forgotten. I will never forget my stare down with a black panther.

ENCOUNTER WITH AN UFO?

The Athens Messenger

OHIO UNIVERSITY LIBRARY

Hocking Valley — ATHENS, OHIO, TUESDAY, MARCH 29, 1966 — *Ohio River Valley* — TEN CENTS

THE WEATHER — Partly cloudy tonight and Wednesday. Warmer tonight. Low tonight in the mid 30s. High Wednesday in the mid 50s.

UFO Spotted Over Athens; Resembles Patrolman's Hat

One night while I was walking home from my friend's house and passing the driveway to this cemetery, all of a sudden, a gigantic light came slowly down from the sky into this cemetery. It was so bright I don't know how anyone could miss it. I bet my hair stood straight up, I was so scared I couldn't move. It was like being held there and forced to watch this light. Once I was able to move, I ran a whole mile to get home and I only slowed up for a rest once. When I did slow up there was a crashing in the woods. If I would have been older, I bet I would have had a heart attack. I thought the light was coming for me so I poured it on and ran as hard as I could. When I got to my Grandma's house I didn't even slow down for the door. It was a good thing she never locked it, and it was hanging open a little, or there would have been no door. As I look back now it probably was a deer that I scared in the woods. I wonder if that deer knew how much he scared me. I have never seen the light since that night. I have no idea what it was.

THE LIGHT
Eyewitness Account

One evening I went to town to pick up a pizza for dinner. It was dark with no moon and very little stars out. I don't usually travel the back roads but on this night I did. I thought it would be quicker to go this way. When returning from town I was just cruising along not thinking about anything important. Suddenly, a bright light was approaching from behind me with great speed. I thought that they would hit me they were traveling so fast. The light got so close and bright it illuminated the inside of my vehicle. Just when I thought it was going to hit me it shot straight up into the night sky. It went so far up that it went out of sight. This UFO was a neat experience, but I wasted no time in getting home. I don't travel that road at night anymore.

SOUNDLESS CRAFTS
Eyewitness Account

During the end of the 1960's, three different eyewitnesses saw a formation of planes flying in the evening sky. From one of the witness accounts these mysterious planes were believed to be UFO's. This is the story told by one of the witnesses. My home is located north of Athens.

It was early evening when I looked up into the sky and saw about seven planes flying in an odd formation. What was unique about them was they were flying low and there was no sound coming from the aircrafts. The planes were black in color. I have never seen or heard of a plane that made no sound when climbing in a high altitude unless they were from another technology not of this world. It was like they had no engines

'FLYING SAUCER?'—Sheriff George Bateman (left) and Dr. John E. Edwards, assistant professor of physics at Ohio University, examine the Rube Goldbergian contraption found Saturday at Millfield, Dr. Edwards pronounced it a hoax.

at all. If I had to guess of what they were I would say they were definitely genuine UFO's. I have looked for years and have never seen anything like them in the sky again.

ENCOUNTERS OF A DIFFERENT KIND
Eyewitness Account

As I was driving home from work one sunny afternoon, I stopped for a red light. I was going to turn left, and I noticed a vehicle approaching me with three occupants, the driver was signaling with his hand to turn left, so we could both turn at the same time when the light turned green. As I was shifting gears and readying to turn, a hand grabbed my arm and a voice said, "Don't believe him!" I was stunned, but sat still, waiting for the other car to proceed with their turn. The driver just gunned his engine and sat facing me. I didn't move my car but waited for the other driver to respond. The light changed to red again, and we both just sat there waiting; there was a vehicle coming up behind me as the light turned green, I proceeded to wait on the oncoming driver. Finally, he didn't turn left, but squealed across the intersection and as he got beside me, he yelled, "Stupid bitch!" and proceeded on his way. I turned left and headed on home. I believe the entity in my car was aware of the actions of the oncoming driver. I was an older female, old enough to remember the hand signaling before signal lights were put on vehicles, I was alone and there were no other vehicles in sight at that time. I had just gotten off work and was anxious to get home; it is possible that I would have turned left, thinking he was going to turn left also. But he was planning on coming straight and then say I turned left in front of him, possibly feigning injury, and damage to his vehicle; he had two witnesses. My car was newer than his, and I'm sure the insurance company would have paid dearly for whatever damage was caused if I had pulled out and turned in front of him. The accident would clearly have appeared to be my fault, he didn't have his turn signal on, and the driver behind me probably couldn't see his hand signal. Therefore, it would appear that I had pulled out in front of the oncoming vehicle, and he had witnesses to prove it. I recognized the voice in my car; I had heard it the winter before while driving to work, but I have never seen the entity where the voice was coming from. Once as I was going to work, the roads were icy in spots. I turned onto Second Street in Athens, going downhill, and the street was a clear sheet of ice. I was sliding all over; my brakes were not doing anything to help. I turned my wheel into the curb on the right of the street and skidded down the hill. As I approached the end of the street, there was a car parked in my path. I nearly panicked!! At about that time, a salt truck turned the corner coming up the hill, leaving salt in the other lane and melting the ice. Somehow, my car stopped against the curb while the truck passed; I was shaking all over, not only from the cold, but also from the frightful situation I was in. then, from out of the blue, a voice said, "Get into the other lane!" I said, "Oh, sure, then a car will come up the hill – what then?" The voice said again, "Get into the other lane, dummy, don't worry, it's okay." My car started skidding again and I turned the wheels into the other lane. I made it down the hill, around the corner, and onto a street that was cleared. I made up my mind that I would never drive to work if the roads were icy again. I made it a habit to wait until the roads were cleared, even if it meant getting to work late. If the schools were closed because of the weather, I didn't go to work. It isn't because I thought my guardian angel wouldn't come to the rescue, but because I felt it only made sense not to drive under conditions that would cause undue anxiety and stress to my angel and me! The voice and language were familiar; I had a name for my guardian angel. Anyway, I believe these were encounters of a different kind, and I do believe in guardian angels.

Mysterious places

These exhibits are on display at the Mothman museum
Point Pleasant, WV

FRIDAY THE 13TH

It is Friday the 13th 2000, tonight there is a full moon for the first time on Friday the 13th in 512 years. It is a cool crisp evening and a perfect time to take the first ever Haunted Athens Tour. This adventure promises to take a tour through the Ridges, formally the Athens Mental Health Center or the Asylum Grounds. Also, we are supposed to see the famed body stain on the fourth floor and later meet in the cemetery for ghost stories. Once we get to the meeting place it seems like it is going to be a normal small group to go. When 9:30 comes around the crowd is so massive it looks like a Kiss concert. There must be thousands of people here for this tour. People can't even move around without running in to someone. So away we all go to the Ridges, everyone especially wants to see the famed body stain on the fourth floor. The masses build on the ridge. There are even more people here than there were at the meeting point. There are so many people gathered that the building maintenance people say that no one is going to be able get in for the tour. The Ohio University police arrive to keep this crowd from getting ugly. When the crowd finally disperses, we decide to walk up to the emetery anyway. When we get there, people are running around, yelling, and tromping all over the graves. Where is the respect for the dead? My first thought is 'I can't believe we have made it to the 21st century.' I have never seen people act like this in a graveyard. Even though the community never got to go in the buildings it was still a neat experience. I myself didn't mind not being able to go in, I had already seen what people wanted to see. I worked for OU when they first started to transform the Asylum Grounds into the Ridges. I was able to walk all around the buildings and see things that the crowd was talking about.

The body stain is really there; it is weird that nothing will clean it up or so that is the rumor. I have been down in the dungeons, or at least that's what I called it, as well. There are great myths that the place is haunted, this I can't say for sure. But I do know it is a very weird feeling to be in the attics or basements. I only wish that my wife and stepdaughter

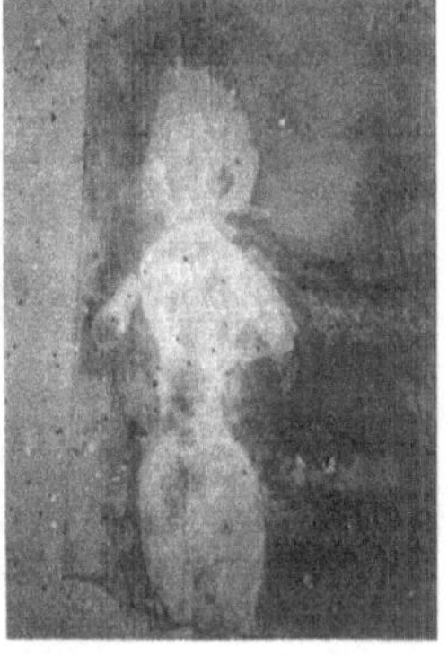

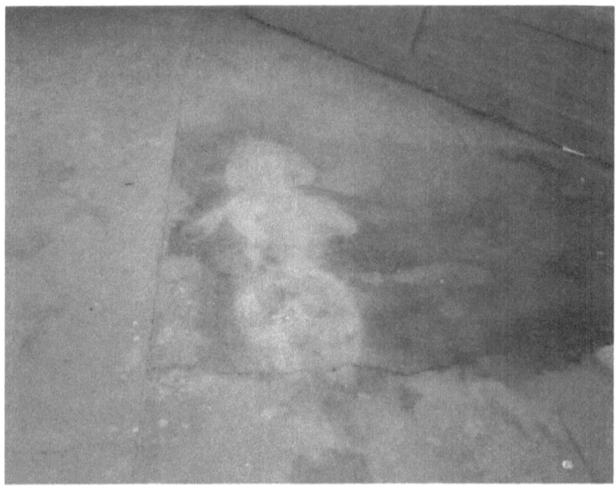

could have seen some of the things I have been able to see up on the ridges. But I guess they will have to read about it and see it on T.V. this month. They can still listen to my stories of going down in the dungeon when I first started working at the ridges. This is only one of Athens most eerie mysteries.

Having lived here all my life I feel fortunate to have seen some of the things most people are only able to talk about.

THE MOTHMAN LEGEND

This little West Virginia town is full of history. There are a few interesting legends like the curse of Chief Cornstalk and the Mothman. There is also the tragic collapse of the Silver Bridge. Chief Cornstalk put a curse on this area with his dying words. There have also been reports of UFO's in this area. The most prominent legend is that of the Mothman. This creature gave the area a lot of attention. Eyewitness accounts of this being were documented in the newspaper article from the Archives & Special Collections Ohio University Libraries This account describes the witness's sightings of this creature in the TNT area (a munitions factory during World War II). This is where the Mothman was first spotted. It was described with two big red eyes and a wingspan of about ten feet and manlike.

IS THERE A MASON COUNTY MONSTER?

Four Witnesses of 'The Bird...(?)' Swear It's True

On the afternoon of December 15th, 1967, the Silver Bridge Collapsed. It was later determined that one of the eye bars was what caused the bridge to collapse. Some wondered if the Mothman or the curse of Cornstalk was responsible for the bridges collapse. After this tragic event the sightings of the Mothman faded away but they were not forgotten. Even in this day the fame of the Mothman is going strong in movies, television, books, and the Internet. I have traveled to Point Pleasant in search of the Mothman legend.

There is not much to be told that hasn't been told already in other books and articles. I just thought it was an interesting legend and worth looking into.

The legend of Chief Cornstalk (Keigh-Tugh-gua) is fascinating too. Shawnee Chief Cornstalk led his people in a military attempt to drive away the settlers. When his campaign failed, he attempted to talk for peace.

Unfortunately, the settlers still harbored bitterness over

the "Battle of Point Pleasant". As a result of these ill feelings, Chief Cornstalk was murdered one night by angry former soldiers. The legend rumors that Chief Cornstalk with his dying words put a two-hundred-year curse on Point Pleasant.

Wreckage of Bridge, Seen From Ohio Side

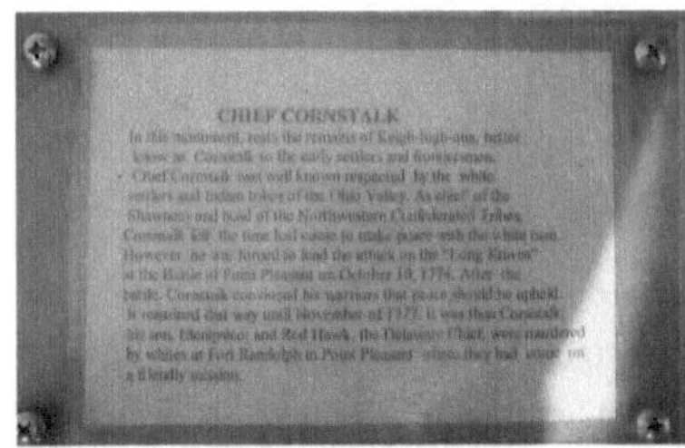

THE WEEPING ANGEL

It was a windy and cool afternoon when we went to visit the cemetery on West State Street, in Athens Ohio. An iron fence guards the cemetery, but the gate is hanging open inviting visitors to come in. The leaves from the trees were covering a lot of the graves like blankets. There is plenty of history in this place, almost all the wars have contributed a person here like the Revolutionary War veterans, service men that were in the War of 1812, and the Civil War, even the veterans of World War I and II.

There is a lot of Athens history buried here. Some we will never know because of the tragic effects of time. There is even a tombstone that a tree grew around. As you enter the gate there is a statue to commemorate the many unknown soldiers that reside here. The statue is that of an angel. It is the statue that has a legend surrounding it. The statue has been reported to shed tears. I looked this statue over really good and it looks like it could have shed tears from the stains under the eyes. It could be stained from the two trees on each side of it. While I was in the cemetery it never shed a tear. I think it has the right to cry from the way the cemetery looks. There were beer cans lying around the statue, someone left a glass hanging over the fence that surrounds it; tombstones are broke in half, and some of them are in three pieces. I do think someone takes care of the cemetery but it's hard to keep vandals out.

I once heard a former college student say, 'You never had

an experience until you have passed out dead drunk in the cemetery.' With all the noise and parties that go on around the cemetery it would wake the dead. If the legend of the angel shedding tears is true, I believe that it has a good cause to shed them. Is this a sign to give the veterans that fought for freedom in the centuries past respect and forever peace for their sacrifice? Or

are they disappointed that no one remembers who they were? Then I wonder if it cries because of the people who have no respect for the dead. Someone has been taking care of the graves and fixing the tombstones or making new markers. Maybe the angel is crying in rejoice that somebody cares.

THE RIDGES

After doing a story about the Ridges another ghost sighting came to my attention. In one of the three cemeteries up at the Ridges is a cemetery that had little access to until recently when stairs were built to get to have easier access from the Dairy Barn. The workers saw a ghost walking through the cemetery.

The three cemeteries have patients of the Athens Mental Health Center (longtime residents of Athens refer to it as the Asylum Grounds) buried in them and some civil war veterans. Most of the graves are just numbers although there are a few names. After reading an article in the Athens News about restoring the cemeteries and the ghost sighting, I had to go back again. With any luck I might get to see this specter. Early on a windy December morning I went to the Ridges cemeteries to have a look around, there was no spook to be found on this morning. It was still a nice morning to wander around for some photos. The Ridges has had its share of ghost sightings and legends throughout the years and is a very popular place for paranormal activity over the years.

 I often wonder if this is the legacy to be remembered the most about the old asylum. After seeing a lot of photos from the Athens Asylum it should be remembered for a lot more than legends, it should just be a part of its heritage.

URBAN LEGENDS

Hanning Cemetery is thought to be one of five cemeteries that form a pentagram around Athens. The other four are Simms, Higgins, Zion, and Cuckler or at least that's the way legend goes. (However, this cemetery is not the one that we thought it was.) A couple of séances have taken place at Hanning; one of them took place in 1969. Hanning is said to be haunted by an unknown man wearing a long robe. You're also supposed to be able to hear screams in the night. There are other references to the cemetery as being used for public executions. I had the opportunity to visit Hanning. It was on a Sunday afternoon in the fall, one week before Halloween. I have been to a couple of the cemeteries that make the pentagram in Athens County, but this was the first time we all were able to go to one of them together. When we got there, it wasn't exactly what we had expected. It's an older cemetery, but not like the others that I have visited. This one has been taken better care of than some of the others. There are newer graves in it unlike in some of the other less kept cemeteries that I have seen. But you can tell it is old due to the trees growing up through the graves. As we ventured on through to the back, I started noticing trees growing through the graves that were different from the rest. There were more cedar trees with lots of branches and knotholes that were more twisted and gnarly looking. We ventured further through taking pictures and looking at the sunken graves and old tombstones. When we reached the back corner of the cemetery, my wife was standing by a grave when she said she felt a cold chill. We couldn't make out a name on the tombstone she was standing by, but the cold spot was there, nonetheless. It was warm that afternoon, so I walked to the spot and I too felt that it was really cold there. It was almost freezing cold, but it only lasted a minute, and then it was gone. I have read of cold spots like the one my wife and I felt in houses that were supposed to be haunted. Now the question is: did we imagine it? My wife says no she never felt anything like it before. I wonder if we actually did come into brief contact with the spirit world. We have experienced other things, so my wife believes we truly did. I personally, still have my doubts and I too have seen some weird things in my life. I'm still not sure about the ghosts, although I have seen them and can't deny the cold spot was there, then gone. The reason we went there was to see if we could find anything, but I think we found a little more than we bargained for. We intend on visiting the pentagram cemeteries as well, but we are also marking them on a map to see if indeed it does hold to the urban legend. Is this cemetery haunted? Who really knows for sure but the ghosts themselves, and the stories that came from there. Someone once mapped these cemeteries to find the pentagram; will we find it to be true or to be just another legend?

THE FORGOTTEN

Upon a ridge top on Peach Ridge there sits a very old cemetery. This cemetery is one of five that forms a pentagram around the Peach Ridge area. The name of it is Slaughter Cemetery. The other four are Simms, Hanning, Hunter, and Matheny. It has been almost forgotten about. The only people who see it are the turkey and deer hunters, that is how I found it many

years ago. This cemetery is well preserved for a forgotten one. There are not any vandals or partiers that get to go there. If you don't know where it is then it is hard to find for it is not on a new map. I found it on a very old map, that's how I drew the pentagram to form around these cemeteries. Now the one thing that I do know from mapping out this pentagram, is that any number of cemeteries can form one on a map. Is this one a coincidence or was it someone in ages past that knew exactly how to plot these ridge tops. I just think it was neat because of the hype Peach Ridge gets because of Simms Cemetery being haunted. One time in the fall, my stepdaughter and I traversed the ridges and briars to get to this place. We thought we might see something in this cemetery. I did not expect to see any spirits or specters. I have turkey hunted right beside this place many times. In the early morning when it's so still out, you could see a ghost for miles or hear one. It is a spooky place just before the sun rises in the morning. Also, it is a beautiful place in the spring mornings after sunrise. I have never seen anything but turkeys and deer around this cemetery.

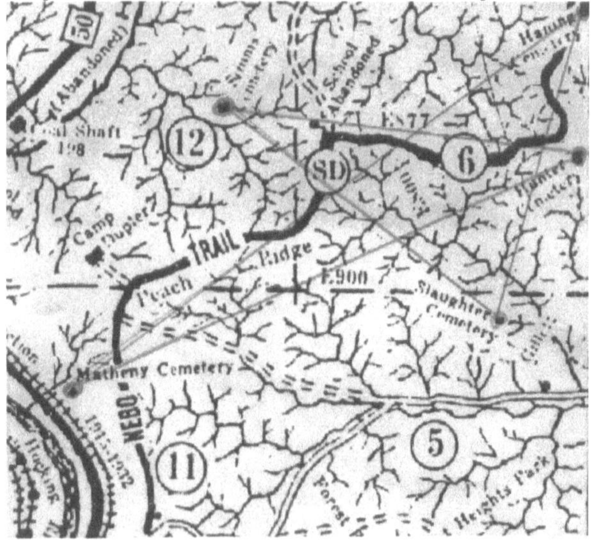

Maybe this is because it is so peaceful out there on that ridge in the middle of nowhere that the ghosts are at peace with no humans to vandalize the cemetery. I think since it is not a well-known cemetery it has not developed any legends of spooks. The residents of this place are long forgotten to ages past. Maybe this is why they don't haunt it. They are resting in eternal and everlasting peace. There is not much to say about this cemetery except it has some beautiful ridges to view the land around it. The last item I have to say is, I hope that this cemetery stays out of reach of housing developments and vandals.

A person cannot speak of the legends in the Athens area without mentioning Mount Nebo, the highest spot in Athens County. The Indians that lived in the area believed that Mount Nebo was sacred ground. The place gained a lot of popularity in the mid-1800s. In that century the idea of contacting the spirit world fascinated the nation. So, a new type of religion was born, it was known as spiritualism. A man named Koons bought the land and formed a group of spiritualists. They performed séances and spoke with the spirits. They constructed a small cabin for their spirit activities to take place. This was the will of the spirits to have this built. The spirits also instructed for paper and pencils to be left in the cabin. There were instructions for musical instruments to be there. A doctor of the time came to visit this place to see if it was real. There were books written about the place and they were passing a good message from the grave. He never charged for his séances. There are reports that hands would move over your body in the services that they performed. There are also reports that spirit-type writings took place without human help. Musical instruments would play beautiful music. It was said that the spirits played the music and it was very loud. The rest of the history says that the local residents started to fear what was going on at Mt. Nebo. It was said they were performing satanic rituals. The locals attacked the house and burnt the people out. The Koons' moved away and were never heard from again. This is how the legend goes; there is a lot of documentation on it. Something went on up there to spook the people, what, I cannot say. Spiritualism is going to spook anyone who doesn't know anything about it. I think if hands were going over my body with no humans doing it, I would be spooked too. I have heard my father tell stories of Mt. Nebo that were passed down from his grandparents. There are also other people who have told the stories of Mt. Nebo. The one thing I do know is there used to be a trail from Athens to Mt. Nebo. I am sure this legend will go on as long as the stories are passed to each generation. How good the stories get with each generation is hard to say. What really happened on Mt. Nebo that spooked the local people? I don't think we will ever know for sure. But I have been to this place and I think it is special, like the Indians believed. There are beautiful views from atop those hills as long as it is like that and the legend goes on it will forever be remembered as a part of the legends in the area.

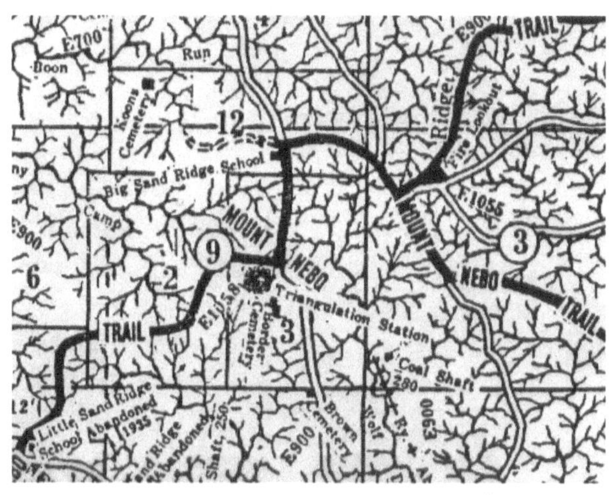
E 700
Run
Boon
Koons Cemetery
12
Big Sand Ridge School
Camp
E 900
6
2
9
MOUNT
NEBO
TRAIL
E 1058
Border Cemetery
3
Little Sand Ridge School
Abandoned 1935
Sand Ridge
Abandoned
Shaft, 250
E 900
Brown Cemetery
Triangulation Station
Coal Shaft
290
Wolf
E 900
By.
Ridge
Fire Lookout
F. 1055
MOUNT
NEBO
TRAIL
3
E 900
TRAIL

THE PENTAGRAM

Legend has it that a pentagram surrounds the city of Athens, Ohio. This legend is a very fascinating part of Athens folklore. The inside of the pentagram is said to be a safety zone in case of some natural catastrophe. It is also said to be a focal point of mystical powers. The pentagram has

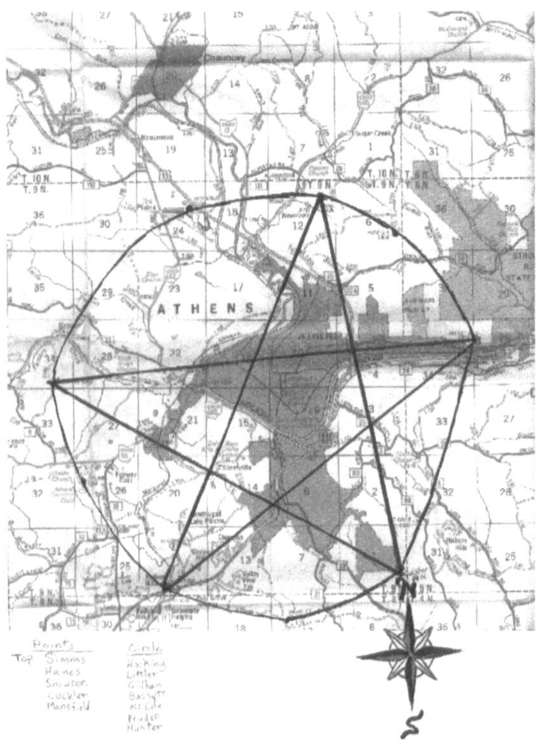

been well documented over the years. There are several different interpretations of the cemeteries that make up the pentagram. I have visited most of the cemeteries concerning this legend. I have written several stories on them in other sections of this book. The cemeteries that have been listed over the years are Simms, Higgins, Zion, Cuckler, Hanning, Hunter, Matheny and even Mt. Nebo as the top point. I have studied old and new maps to plot the pentagram. Starting with Simms as the top point, the rest are Haines, Snowden, Cuckler, and Mansfield. Hocking, Littler, Gilham, Basset, Mc Cole, Pruden and Hunter form the circle. Everyone seems to have his or her own ideas about the pentagram.

The one common thing that never seems to change is that Wilson Hall on the west green of the Ohio University campus is the center of the pentagram. One interesting thing I heard about the ground where Wilson Hall is that it used to be a burial ground. A student also died in Wilson Hall. There have been reports of supernatural incidents that have happened in this building that is in the center of the pentagram. The pentagram I mapped is my interpretation and views of it. I am sure anyone who has studied this legend has their own views about it.

INFAMOUS LEGEND OF BETHEL

Another infamous legend of Athens is Bethel Cemetery in nearby Troy Township. The cemetery is located near the west border of Athens County and is noted for the eerie way in which the graves are laid out. In most cemeteries, the graves are laid in an east to west direction. For centuries the church has followed the tradition of burying the dead looking east facing the rising sun. At Bethel Cemetery, a few of the graves that are said to be more than a hundred years old are inexplicably laid out in a north to south direction; this is the direction of the witch haven of Summerland. Each person's idea of the perfect place to rest and reflect has a personal preference. In Summerland it's the witches. This is how the legend is told. My wife and I went to visit Bethel Cemetery one November afternoon. We were checking to see if the graves do indeed face north to south; that much of the legend is true. A weird thing happened when we got out of our vehicle, a large gust of freezing wind blew so hard you couldn't catch your breath. It was like it was blowing us back away from the cemetery. Since it was November a person would expect freezing wind, but it was a relativity calm day. Were we being pushed away from the cemetery?

Who knows? When we walked through the cemetery looking for these graves it didn't look much different than any other cemetery. We couldn't find them until I got my compass out, then they really stood out from the rest of the graves. The one that stood out the best was so weathered from the effects of time; it had washed almost all traces of who was buried in the grave away.

I don't know about Summerland, but the graves were turned different than the rest of them. Was it done by accident or was it planned that way? That is for someone else to decide. I am just telling the story, and this was my experience when we were checking out the legend.

STILL WATCHING OVER THE FURNACE

It was sometime around mid-1860's when the iron ore industry was thriving. It is a cold chilly evening. There is a thunderstorm rolling in with lightning flashing, lighting up the sky. There is a furnace, which burns night and day. All the workers have gone home after a long day's work, except for one, a night watchman who guards the furnace. He walks around the furnace platform where the iron ore is being melted. All of a sudden a flash of lightning strikes close, he screams as he falls into the bubbling inferno.

The man becomes a victim to the super-hot molten iron ore. This all happened in what is now the Lake Hope State Park. In this century, all that remains of the iron ore industry and the furnace are scattered remains. The watchman still remains to guard the furnace that he perished in, an inconceivable death. On the remaining edge of the furnace, a person can still see his outline and maybe the lantern, still patrolling his furnace. The watchman is best seen on a rainy and stormy night. This is the legend that has been passed through the generations. I went to visit the furnace site at Lake Hope State Park. It started out to be a perfect evening, it was rainy and cool. We got there just before dark to take some photos.

We were in hopes that the watchman would appear on this rainy evening. The only incident that occurred that evening was some hikers coming back to their car. Is there a furnace spook? Well, we wouldn't find out on this outing, but maybe the next time. There have been a lot of reports of it being seen. Will he show the next time we visit? I hope so he has had to show to some people, and I hope our time is the next time we visit the furnace. There are too many rumors or sightings of the watchman showing for it not to have happened at least once to someone. Is this just a myth or is there really something out at the furnace?

The Hope Furnace is a nice historical place to visit.

THE EMMITT HOUSE

The year 1861 could have been one of the most distressing years in this nation's history. This was during the civil war and the nation was in chaos. It was also in this year that James Emmitt started construction on his hotel in the town of Waverly, Ohio. When the Emmitt House was finished it gained a reputation as one of the Scioto Valley's best hotels. Railroads took place of the Ohio-Erie Canal in the 1860's, and in the late 1870's. The Scioto Valley Railroad and the Ohio Southern each ran several trains through Waverly daily. The Emmitt House operated a horse-drawn bus which met each train, carrying passengers to and from the Emmitt House. Hotel guests could also take the bus to performances at Emmitt's

Opera House on Walnut Street. The Opera House, converted from a Catholic church in 1875, offered traveling drama & musical troops on a monthly basis well into the 1890's. It was a center for all kinds of salespeople and a major attraction even in this day and age. The Emmitt House remains a living memorial to James Emmitt a century later. The Emmitt House was restored in 1989, the historical look was retained. The house is listed on the National Register of Historical Places.

There is another aspect to The Emmitt House, a legend that it is haunted. Here are some of the instances of things that have happened there. Pam Justice told us of these sightings and happenings. One morning the Pepsi vendor tried to get into the Emmitt House, but he couldn't figure why the people wouldn't let him in. Pam told him that she was the first one to arrive at the house. The Pepsi man told her he had seen a woman in a cleaning outfit upstairs. Pam told him that no one cleans upstairs, and no one is on the payroll to do that. He described her to be wearing a cleaning outfit of times gone by. Pam said, "Do you think anyone in this day and age wears a cleaning outfit"? The weird thing about the second and third floors of the Emmitt House is a person hardly ever sees cobwebs. Pam has worked there for over ten years and has never seen very many cobwebs on those floors. This seems unusual for such an old building. The people who work at the bank drive thru have told that they have seen a cleaning lady on the second floor in the windows. This could happen in the day or night. One person had an office on the second floor and there were several times she was pecked on the shoulder by something, but she never seen anyone do it. There have also been sightings of a little girl down by the bar. This has happened on several occasions. In one of the rooms on the second-floor people has smelled cigar smoke. After hearing about the Emmitt House, I had to go see it. Four of us went on this excursion to see if we could find a ghost in the Emmitt House. In one of the halls something pushed me. It was in the hall next to the room where the cleaning lady has been seen. What pushed me, I have no idea because no one was close to me. The feeling in this hall was very intense and I had to leave for a while. All four of us had some kind of eerie experience while we were upstairs. I did notice that there were no cobwebs on this floor. I didn't know about the cleaning lady until after I had gone through this hall. Cold spots are all over the upstairs of the Emmitt House. Every one of us had noticed them. We had smelled the cigar smoke in a room on the second floor. When we went to the third floor Vikki did not want to be up there. She was pushed backwards at the top of the stairs going to the third floor. She had some very intense feeling of something watching her. In almost every photo there was some kind of anomaly. Were we touching the spirit world?

The staff at the Emmitt House was very nice to be

around. The food was great, and it is a nice place to visit. There is a lot of history at the Emmitt House. The Emmitt House is located at North Market Street Waverly, Ohio Just off of state route 23. I hope to go back soon and if we don't see a ghost at least we can have a good meal. Editor's note: Since the initial publication of this story, the Emmitt House was lost to fire on January 7th, 2014. It was a total loss. Was it caused by the cigars we smelled? You decide.

THE GHOST TOWN OF SAN TOY

Perry County, Ohio is the location of a once booming mining town called San Toy. The Sunday Creek Coal Company Mine No.1 and Mine No.2 were located in this area. The town had a theater, hospital, and saloons. The coal mine was the heart of the town. It is said that shootouts took place in the streets of this settlement. This town was a lively place in its day. All that remains in this century is foundations and what looks like a jailhouse and of legends of a once wild booming town.

All that can be seen now is the ghost of a once prominent mining town. As we were visiting San Toy and walking through this ghost town our little group took several pictures. I have often wondered if specters still walk the long-gone streets of this once proud mining town. None was to be seen when we visited but who is to say that when the midnight hour strikes that life or echoes from the past might still show up in this ghost town.

MILLFIELD: A SMALL TOWN
Full of History

This Appalachian town has had its share of the spotlight over the years. Mine Disaster! UFO crash! Train wrecks! The town had national spotlight on November 5, 1930 when the Sunday Creek Mine No.6 had an explosion of gas, the blazing inferno trapping several hundred men.

Ambulances were quickly gathered for emergency work after news of the calamity spread, as is testified in the above photo.

The mine was abandoned in the 1940's, but there still remains traces of it slowly disappearing with the years. The only thing that is visible now is the smokestack. This tragedy is the worst mine disaster in Ohio mining history. The explosion at this mine took 82 lives. The historical marker that is at the site reads: MILLFIELD COAL MINE DISASTER NOVEMBER 5, 1930 Ohio's worst mine disaster occurred in this Sunday Creek Coal Company mine when an explosion killed 82 persons. Among the dead were the company's top executives who were in the mine inspecting new safety equipment. Nine hours after the explosion, rescuers discovered 19 miners alive underground three miles from the main shaft.

The disaster attracted national press coverage and international attention, and it prompted improvement of Ohio's mine safety laws in 1931. About the time the incident at Roswell, New Mexico happened something landed in the grass at the Millfield Post Office. A UFO? It was dismissed as a hoax. Maybe with everyone being a little disturbed about Roswell, things were always falling out of the sky. The Underground Railroad legacy also resides in Millfield. As is with much of southeastern Ohio. There have been several train wrecks in Millfield over the century. After visiting the mine disaster site, a person would think it would be haunted after the tragedy that had taken place. We never had that feeling there and if it is haunted no one is talking, not even the spirits.

PAYNE'S CROSSING

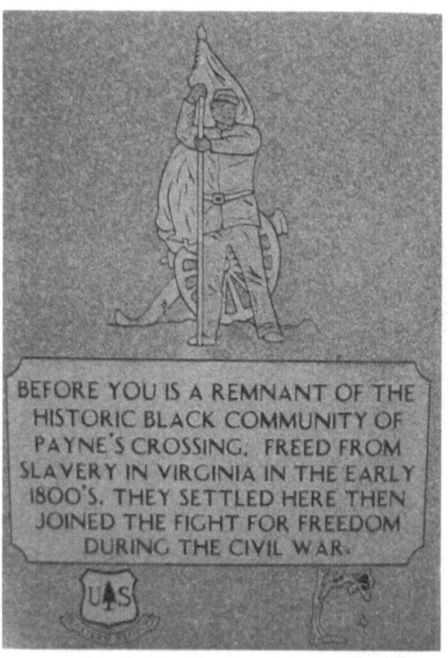

One afternoon while out driving around looking for a legend or ghost story to investigate and I could write about, I came to the Hocking and Perry county line. There sitting on top of this hill was Payne's Cemetery. Thinking maybe I might find something interesting I stopped. There were a lot of old graves found there and the interesting marker at the front of the cemetery. After I left, I couldn't get this place out of my mind, so my wife and I went back. Then I headed to the library to see what kind of history was here. Payne's Crossing was a community of escaped slaves. This was also a stopping place for the Underground Railroad. This cemetery was abandoned for a long time. The Wayne National Forest cleaned it up and turned it into a historical site. Maybe this will do honor for the ones buried there. The town around this area seems to be a mystery. Or was there a town?

There is a lot of history buried there and that is where legends begin.

THE GHOST OF THE ISLAND

The Blennerhassett Mansion

Harman and Margaret Blennerhassett a couple of aristo-crats came to North America in the late 1700's and to the island a couple of years later. The mansion was completed in 1800. Due to their involvement with Aaron Burr, the Blennerhassetts moved from the island and the original mansion burnt to the ground. The state of West Virginia rebuilt the house into a tourist attraction. But there are stories of Margaret Blennerhassett being seen there in this day and age. After hearing of this I decided to go and see if her spirit could be seen. After taking a tour of the mansion and the island she was not to be seen on this day. Maybe she did not want to be seen! The visit to the island was nice.

LEGENDS AT THE FORT

This might seem like a history lesson about Old Fort Niagara, it is located a few miles from Niagara Falls at the end of the Niagara River and Lake Ontario. I was fortunate enough to visit this historic fort on a trip to Niagara Falls. The area was visited by the French explorer La Salle in 1678. There is also a castle built by the French around 1725. This old fort has seen a lot of history throughout the years by the British, French and American people. Several battles were fought there, even during the Civil War it was manned in case of possible invasion from forces on behalf of the Confederate states. One thing that interested me besides all of the history was a legend of a haunted well. The legend is that two French officers were dueling and one of them was beheaded. His body was tossed into the well, and his head threw into Lake Ontario. The well was sealed to be uncovered later. It is said that the ghost at Fort Niagara still walks the castle in search of his head.

There are several legends surrounding Fort Niagara. The haunted well was my favorite. The visit to the Fort was the highlight of the trip. I would like to go back around Halloween instead of the early fall when I was there. It is great spot for anyone to visit when traveling.

JACK O' LANTERN

I have written about a light that appears in the woods on our property in previous tales. This light could be something that is mentioned in British folklore called will o' the wisp or jack o' lantern. It is also called Ignis Fatuus which is Latin for foolish fire. According to folklore will o' the wisp was associated with spirits of the dead that couldn't enter heaven or hell. One of today's explanations for this kind of light could be ball lightening. These lights have been appearing all over the world for untold ages. The most famous one in southeastern Ohio is at the Moonville tunnel. The light that appears on our farm happens on rainy nights; it glows really bright then fades out. In the spring of 2002, it is still there. I had watched this light for a while one evening. The more it is seen the more curiosity it causes to arise.

The next night about 9:30 in the evening we decided to go and hunt the ghost light to see what this light could be that has appeared for more than a hundred years. The last time it was looked for was about 35 years ago. My Dad went to look to see what it was. I decided to pick up his trail and check it out myself.

When the hour turned to 10:00pm, my stepdaughter, her boyfriend, Brad, and I decided to go. It was a very dark night with no moonlight to guide us to our destination. So, with our flashlights, cameras, and curiosity we headed for the woods where the light has been seen for so long. Once we got there, we could hear the creatures of the night making their noises. Maybe it was my imagination but there were other noises too. It was almost like someone walking ahead of us.

We started down the hill when this tree caught my eye. We started taking pictures around this area. I took a photo of the tree and something white went straight up into the air. That really made things even more eerie. This tree seemed to be a focal point of strange happenings. We wandered through these woods for a little while longer. It seemed the longer we were there the more tense everyone's feelings got. Upon returning home and looking over the photos the strange things that I saw appeared on the pictures. We looked at the rest of the photos and some orbs appeared in them as well as something else that looked like sprites. There were little lights that were all around us. Being the skeptic that I am I wondered if the little lights were bugs? After viewing the photos, I had picked up flying bugs and they are totally different from the lights that we had seen. This was an interesting adventure and I hope we all have the chance to go back together and figure out what the little lights are. The next day my wife and I went to the same tree that had produced the vortex the night before. "I stood back away from the tree so my husband could set up the camera on the tripod. While I was standing there watching him, I felt something very cold on my arm just below my elbow and above my wrist. I looked down and saw nothing. I felt as though I was frozen there. The wind was not blowing and no other part of my arm, fingers or face felt this sensation. I finally found the courage to tell my husband of this feeling. He turned the camera around to me and took a picture. After that I walked around a little bit. Later I returned to the same spot, but the coldness was not there. We later looked at the photos and nothing showed up beside me. Was the feeling my imagination or something wanting to hold me there?" We went back to this spot-on Halloween night of 2002, to see if weird things would once again show in the photos. I guess there is nothing weird about a ring of trees except it was brought to my attention that this ring appears to be a fairy ring. This is from more folklore just like will-o'-the wisp. If the legends of folklore are true, then maybe this light is will-o'-the wisp or just a foolish light.

AIRPLANE HOLLOW

This legend is in the hills of Southeastern Ohio in Hocking County. Sometime in the 1950s a plane crashed with 50 or so passengers. This is how the legend goes; not much information is given on the facts of this crash except it is now called Airplane Hollow. The crash caused a big fire which destroyed a lot of the area. Mangled bodies were lying over the hillside. Now some sixty years later when walking up Airplane Hollow the ghostly apparitions of the doomed plane are still haunting the hillside. I have traveled through Airplane Hollow and it is kind of creepy even in the daytime.

On top of the ridge is a cemetery called the Bone Yard. The Bone Yard is rumored to be haunted. It is not as hair-raising there as one would think a haunted cemetery would be. I wonder if the specters from the crash site are what haunts the area. Maybe the cemetery is as close as they can get to their final resting place in Airplane Hollow.

APPARITION MAKES PUBLIC LIBRARY HOME

The history of the current Portsmouth Public Library building all began on January 18, 1902, when Henry Lorberg made a formal request to the Carnegie Corporation. Once his request was received a response was returned noting that the officials in charge of the Carnegie foundation grants were giving careful thought to the Portsmouth request. Then on February 9, 1902, word came in an article appearing in the New York Times stating that Andrew Carnegie had chosen Portsmouth as one of the cities in which to build a library. Since that time, the grand structure has come a long way, as the original building has undergone two additions, the first in 1971, and the second completed in 1995. As with any historic establishment anything is bound to happen, and possibilities are somewhat endless as well. So, with this said, it has been rumored that the Portsmouth Public Library has been home to its own apparition. However, do ghosts really exist? Many believe they walk among us, although most of us cannot see or hear them. Then again, some people believe that ghostly phenomenon only occurs late at night, around old buildings or churchyards. Nonetheless, this particular spirit seems to be quite comfortable and content. One might even say she is quite the discrete patron... you hardly ever notice she's around.

ABOUT THE AUTHOR

Lawrence Everett, has been a life-long resident of Athens County, Ohio. He is an avid outdoorsman, comic book collector, artist and ghost hunter. He has spent many years delving into the folklore of the region and visiting the sites represented in "Ghostly Legends".

For more information about this book and Mr. Everett, visit, everett.stormgatepress.com

www.ingramcontent.com/pod-product-compliance
Lightning Source LLC
Chambersburg PA
CBHW060540160726
47991CB00001B/400